Praise for *Bigger Than Jesus*

*In the first book of The Hit Man Series, Cuban hit
man Jesus Diaz battled New York's Spanish mob to escape
the thug life with stolen mafia money and the lovely Lily
Vasquez.
Read Bigger Than Jesus, the book that started the
series.*

"Bigger than Jesus is wickedly real and violently
funny."
~ *Claude Bouchard, bestselling author of Vigilante*

Reviews of *Bigger Than Jesus*

"This new thriller by the author of *Self-Help for
Stoners* is a crime story worthy of Elmore Leonard with a
backstory that is shades of Thomas Harris.
An unusual mix of some stock characters and a
gangland scenario which is made fresh by great,
punchy dialogue and plot twists that keep you moving
from one calamity to the next with no time to catch your
breath…"

"This can't-wait-to-discover-how-he-gets-out-of-this-
situation nail biter will keep you entertained to the last
page!"

"With *Bigger Than Jesus*, Robert Chazz Chute proves
that genre fiction can be inventive and unconventional in

its use of language while delivering a suspenseful story."

"With comedy throughout and a wonderful cast of characters, *Bigger Than Jesus* pulled me right in and wouldn't let me go."

"At times it has the brutal violence that I expect from crime novels, but mostly it is funny.
Jesus Dias has a sharp tongue and it seems that he modelled his life after Mike Hammer from Micky Spillane's books and after numerous characters he has seen in movies."

"For a murder book, the way it was written had me smiling through it, the scene on the roof had me laughing. It was a light and enjoyable
mob mystery."

"I enjoyed the twists and turns of this novel and was not able to put it down until I read the whole thing."

Reviews of *Higher Than Jesus*
In Higher Than Jesus, our luckless hit man is on the run from The Machine and the FBI in Chicago. Hard to say which will kill him first, the Vicodin addiction, the gang members or the gun runners.

"Jesus is a bad guy you hate to love."

"In between all the funny cultural references is a solid, well-plotted crime thriller that is thoroughly enjoyable from start to finish. There is nothing slow or dull about this book.
So do we need yet another series about a hit man?

Only if it's about Jesus Diaz."

"A quick-moving plot with lots of surprises and a clear-eyed examination of addiction."

DEDICATION

Hollywood Jesus
Rise of the Divine Assassin
Robert Chazz Chute

Published by Ex Parte Press
ISBN 978-1-927607-03-9

Dedication
She Who Must Be Obeyed makes it all possible.
The prince and princess make it all worth it.

Acknowledgements
Many people have donated their time and energy to
help make my books a reality. To
Kit Foster of Kit Foster Design, Armand Rosamilia,

Mark Victor Young, Janice Kurita, Brian Wright, RCMP
Cst. Leland Keane, Russ Sawatsky, Susan Toy, Claude
Bouchard, Johanna Goldenberg, Alex Kimmell, Tidal
Ashburn, Mazie Lane and Peter Hawkins:
Thank you all so much for your support.

RT ALPHABET AGENCIES: YOU GUYS NEED TO BUY BETTER SUITS. YOU ALL LOOK ALIKE. @ASSASSINSPLAYBK

When numerous alphabet agencies hunt you, it is best to keep a low profile.

Rule #1: Avoid the limelight's burn.

Rules #2 and #3 are to eschew drama's sting and to duck trauma's pain. You didn't do that and now, here you are. The FBI agent on the floor is face-down dead and the bad guy, Detective Hank Reles, has a gun — *your* SIG Sauer P220 — aimed at your forehead. Worse? This is not at all how you'd planned to tear up Hollywood. It's apparent you have failed, again, to observe the rules of *The Divine Assassin's Playbook*. You made up those rules. You'll die for it.

"Take out your phone, Mr. Diaz," Reles says.

With shaking hands, you do as you're told.

"Call her," he says.

"I wouldn't. It won't do you any good."

"Call her or I'll kneecap you and then you'll call her anyway, but crying hard." He takes a step closer. He gestures with the pistol, urging you to hurry.

If you call and she answers, you're pretty sure he'll empty his magazine into you without a blink.

What will your obituary read? Possibly: "Originally from Cuba and a former Military Policeman, Jesus Salvador Umberto Luis Diaz was largely misunderstood and he didn't mean to get into the assassin and vengeance-for-hire business. He killed a lot of bad people but leaves no legacy besides death. In his heart, he was always pure. Sometimes he actually thought he served Justice. But hey, shit happens."

"Now!" the big man roars.

You take a deep breath, squeeze your eyes tight and three...two...one....you hit *Send*.

Is this all there is? Time to find out. You open your mouth, but not to speak.

This is how it ends.

* * *

Your story starts, if any story can be said to have one beginning, with a call from your boss, friend and Ving Rhames lookalike, Chillie Gillie.

"Who's the client?"

Chill won't say, so you know the client is a friend — an even better friend than you. When pressed, Chill admits the client is "tight like family, so I need you for an extra-special, special project."

Chill's lisp makes it, "extra-spethial, spethial."

"Okay, shoot."

2

"I need you to find something on a guy named Oswald. But no shooting."

"What'd Oswald do besides take the fall for assassinating Kennedy?"

Chill tells you what address to go to and leaves it at that, maybe thinking you won't notice your question went unanswered.

"That's in Montecito. That's not the book depository in Dallas. What did Oswald do?"

"Maybe nothing, but that's not the way to bet. All we know for sure is he's an asshole. This is a search for evidence, off-the-books deal. Go in, but he's a raccoon, not a cockroach, you hear? Don't be a hard rock."

This is Dirty Tricks Department shorthand: raccoons you trap. Cockroaches require extermination.

Knowing your history, Chill feels he needs to drive the point home. "This is *not* a search and destroy mission. Recon, only, you dig?"

"Recon the raccoon. I dig, Shaft."

"Shut your mouth."

"What? Just haven't heard anybody say 'dig' in a long time."

"I'm bringing it back. I'm also thinking of bringing back the word 'groovy'."

"Groovy. I can dig it."

"There you go. But, seriously, you don't have to pull your pistol out every time, man. Use a little finesse."

You end the connection and leave your regular phone with Sgt. Billy. If you're caught, nothing ties you to Chill. That's standard Dirty Tricks Department policy. The entire department is you, but you stick by your rules. Chill gave you a job when no one else would. You owe, therefore you pay.

Sgt. Billy pours black coffee into a thermos. The coffee is sour and stiff, perfect for a long drive and a long wait. Black bag jobs are mostly boring recon followed by a few frantic minutes of anxiety or even terror.

"Big job?" Sgt. Billy asks.

"Maybe, Chill was light in detail so either he doesn't know enough or he knows it could turn into a shit storm. He says I can keep my bullet in my chest pocket so all's quiet on the Western front tonight."

"I'm old enough to get the Barney Fife in Mayberry reference, Jesus, but the Western Front thing — "

"War movie."

"Oh."

The old man will watch pretty much any show with you. You've got a voracious appetite for anything on the old movie channel. However, Sgt. Billy doesn't watch war movies. *Platoon* gave him flashbacks.

Billy hands you the burrito he's cooked on the hotplate, shovelled into a roll of newspaper. "Don't be out too late. I worry." He smiles. "Now gimme a dollar."

You give him a man-hug — one arm clasped low to avoid any chance of accidental pelvic grind, the other goes high to clap him on the back. "Thanks, Mom."

He pushes you away. "Just stay out of trouble, you little monster."

"Staying out of trouble is not the business we're in." You had practiced that in the mirror a few times. You looked good saying it, but Hollywood never calls for you to star in a movie. Hollywood only needs you for raccoons in the garbage and cockroaches under the bed.

You're Jesus Diaz, once a hit man and now in charge of

black bag gigs for Chill's security outfit. You keep the stalkers away. You tell yourself your assassin-for-hire days are over. You haven't completely ruled out knocking off anybody who deserves a long dirt nap, though. This is Hollywood.

It's a beautiful place where aspiring gods and goddesses can live, however briefly, in the sun. But raccoons and cockroaches and agents are everywhere.

RT IF THE TREES ARE DYING, IT'S A MOTH LAB. @ASSASSINSPLAYBK

From your black Ford Fairlane, you watch Oswald's house, a big Spanish villa constructed of pink stucco and bad taste. He doesn't appear to have any domestic servants around the place. You would have watched longer, but it's a nice neighborhood. Hesitate too long and a police cruiser might roll up on you, patroling the nice white neighborhood for unfamiliar brown people. You've got fake ID, of course, but you're too well-dressed to claim you're the gardener waiting for Oswald's return.

Stage One: Look for something incriminating outside the house. The nearby trees aren't dying so the villa is not a meth lab. The windows aren't all blacked out and the curtains aren't all pulled shut so it's not a marijuana grow op. So far, the place looks like all the other big houses down the block except no basketball nets and bicycles litter the driveway. This could be a neighborhood filled with orthodontists and their families.

A few minutes later, you get the text from Chill on your throwaway phone. To dodge tracking, he sends it through an anonymous remailer account. Chill says the client is anxious and in a hurry and you need to do this recon "with alacrity".

"Alacrity?" you text back.

"Hurry da fuck up, in & out, report."

Like all orders, that demand proves inconvenient. You're elbow deep in Oswald's garbage at the back of the house trying to find something useful. So far, his worst crime is that he does not recycle. The state of California doesn't execute non-recyclers unless they are serial offenders. Time to casually fracture a few laws. You begin Stage Two of the recon.

On TV, the hero slips a credit card into the edge of a door to pick a lock. That destroys the credit card — who needs that hassle unless it isn't your card? Also, that isn't nearly as easy as it looks except with old doors at cheap motels. The next option is to pull out a lock pick set and get to work, hoping a nosy neighbor doesn't spot you while you struggle to overcome the lock.

That's not just picky work. It's nit-picky and plenty of locks are different so you have to take the time to learn each lock. More hassle. If television episodes went down in real time, they'd be longer and even more boring.

You've used the hockey stick and bicycle chain trick to rip off doorknobs, but since you'd look suspicious walking around with that sort of bulge under your sports jacket, you've left that tool at home. That's your only complaint about West Coast weather: The sun always shines in California. No stylish trench coat concealing bulky tools of the trade for you.

Nineteen Eighty-four has come to the Golden State and Big Brother is watching. Between the LAPD and wandering bands of TSA VIPR teams — Visible Intermodal Prevention & Response — a brownish fellow like you wearing a heavy trench in the sunshine would be marked for interrogation and a search. It would be grossly unjust, but Homeland Security would send you back to Cuba forever if they had the chance. If they found out your real identity, you'd end up on the Gitmo/water-boarding end of the island, not the cheap tourist destination side.

Why, you wonder again, would Bush call it Homeland Security? The term reeks of Nazis, fascists, *"unt zee Fazaland."* The chief tormentor of your childhood, Tia Marta, had a thick German accent. Plus, you had your fill of real Nazis back in Chicago. Maybe you're a little sensitive on that subject.

Focus. What are you going to do about Oswald's back door?

Keeping a low profile and being a smart ninja requires finesse. If you were a brainless thug, the quickest way into Oswald's house would be to make sure your heel connects full force by the lock and kick it in. That's almost always effective. Paranoid homeowners may spend a grand on a security door, but everybody spends the least they can on the installer so the frame is $25 worth of wood and the screws that hold it in place are usually way too short. One or two kicks would get you in quicker than fumbling with a key.

An amateurish B&E makes plenty of noise, though. That choice could end badly: Nosy neighbor appears, garden trowel still in hand. You've got a rule about keeping civilians safe from the secret war so you'd smile and try to bluff your way past him.

Suppose the old man repays your consideration by sticking the blade of his garden trowel in your throat. Or, you tie up the nosy old man from next-door with the electrical cord from his hedge trimmer. Suppose you ask him politely to shut up while you go about your mission. One heart attack later, that's another murder charge against you. Who needs it?

The key to a happy life is less stress, so you do the brainy thug thing: you look. The key isn't under the mat or on top of the doorframe. It's under the second flower pot you check. The homeowner would have had half a chance of keeping you out a little longer if he'd thought to stick the spare key in the pot's dirt. That would have stymied you easily, but since no one wants dirty fingernails, a moment later you're standing in Oswald's house.

RT BIG IN JAPAN: AWESOME SONG BY ALPHAVILLE @ASSASSINSPLAYBK

As you step into the living room, a motion detector shines red and a shrill alarm goes off, jangling your nerves. However, alarms are even easier to deal with than people who leave their house keys in predictable places. It's the sort of alarm system where a little box makes a big whoop. Then an agent from the alarm company calls to warn you that police are on the way so you better identify yourself or they'll be really mad.

The police, of course, are not on their way. That's a stupid bluff. Homeowners get charged for false alarms so alarm companies don't call 911 unless they're sure somebody's in the house who shouldn't be. Besides, though the LAPD claims a response time of 5.7 minutes, you'd have to be skinning a live puppy while tossing grenades at a nunnery to get attention that fast. For burglaries, the cops might take an hour or not show up at all. Lucky you.

You pull the switchblade from your sock and cut the wires to the little box. The alarm company's agent will still get through to the phone, but all they can do is leave a concerned message on voicemail. With no connection through the alarm box, they'll assume the alarm is bogus since there's no burglar to scold. The LAPD charges $115 for each false alarm, so the alarm company's default is caution. The security system company doesn't want to lose a subscriber, never mind that a charge of $115 for a false alarm is couch change to a guy who owns a house worth many millions. Oswald must be rolling in long paper.

Alarms easily defeated with a knife? You don't worry about those too much. Dogs, you worry about. However, Oswald doesn't have a dog. He has fish, mostly angels and yellow tangs, hanging in place or swimming in slow circles amid coral.

You've heard fish have such short memories, a fish tank may as well be the ocean. To the fish, the ocean floor is littered every few feet with armies of scuba divers standing beside pirate chests spewing oxygen bubbles. Civilians are like that, you suppose. Every day looks the same — their routines, their beliefs, their lives of habit and the expectation they'll get to do it all again tomorrow. Most people seem to forget why they're here, hanging in place and swimming in slow circles.

Each day is different for you, but maybe it would be nice to forget the past, to believe in permanence. It would be good to have something nine to five and reliable to depend upon. Instead, you wander through the rooms of a stranger's house, counting four huge aquaria and wondering what you're supposed to find.

The first to-do on your list is to make sure you have an alternate exit. That's the smart ninja strategy. However, you pause to take in the rich decor: leather furniture, a

11

long marble countertop in the huge kitchen, marble everything in the bathrooms. It's irritating when assholes have such nice things. Your third-floor flop is an old industrial warehouse, empty except for you, Sgt. Billy and the run down Japanese restaurant on the first floor.

The restaurant is called Big in Japan, but that's a lie. It was never big in Japan. The waiter tells you the name is stolen from a fancy restaurant in Montreal. The owner tells you he got it from a song released in 1984 by a forgotten German band called Alphaville. You believe the owner because, though the old cook is a little bent and slow now, when he talks about dancing in hot clubs in Holland over thirty years ago, he gets a wistful look in his eyes.

You run across a table piled with mail. It's a federal offence to read someone else's mail, so you're really in trouble now, mister.

Ross Oswald III is an accountant for a firm that serves some of Hollywood's biggest stars or, as everyone from waiters and car wash slaves to top Scientologists say here, Oswald is "in the Industry." You suspected this already because Oswald's mailbox reads: Ross Oswald III, *Esquire*. There you have it: plenty of independent corroboration he's a douchebag.

Usually, that alone wouldn't be enough to require your skill set. You've often considered going on a rampage — especially when LA traffic pokes at whatever gland in your brain is responsible for road rage. Who in L.A. hasn't had those dark thoughts on the 405?

Realistically, taking down or knocking off every jerk in Hollywood would be a round the clock job for an army. Besides, it would also eliminate a good chunk of on-screen talent, some of the directors and all of the agents. The continued functioning of the world's entertainment machine depends on your restraint. If you destroy Hollywood, that leaves Bollywood to take over the world, and no one wants that. Too much weird, happy dancing.

In an amateur B&E, the desperate crackhead runs straight for the master bedroom, rips out the sock drawer and fills it with valuables and is out and running down the street in two minutes. You're a pro, so you take it slow and check the office off the foyer. The computer is, of course, left on all day so you plug in a jump drive and check his internet history. You don't have to be a hotshot hacker to get into anyone's computer. You just have to walk into their home and be nosy.

No real surprises, but Oswald's got enough kinky porn on his hard drive to tire out a teenaged boy whose parents are away for the weekend. It's the mean bondage stuff that makes you uncomfortable, like your soul wears tight shoes on the wrong feet. You got introduced to BDSM as a kid and seeing it again puts you back in that basement in Miami, sweating.

On your first day in America, you watched your family drown. After the Bug Man kidnapped you off Surfside Beach, you survived slavery for three years. Bludgeoning Tia Marta with a heavy silver tray was step one in your emancipation. You strangled her with the necklace that held the key to your escape. The Bug Man disappeared forever.

You left Miami with a duffel full of clothes, a SIG Sauer P220, a switchblade and Tia Marta's newest pet, little Denny De Molina. You still carry the pistol, the switchblade and a taste for vengeance.

Oswald's porn sites turn your stomach — what happened to porn where no one gets slapped, gagged or strangled? Regular sex on camera is soft core nostalgia from a more innocent time when both partners looked like they were having a good time. The nasty stuff reminds you too much of Tia Marta hurting you. For her, pain was sex.

Clicking through numerous directories, it's not like Oswald has a file folder on his desktop that reads: "Stuff that will put me away for life" or "Lord Vader's Nefarious Plans for the Death Star." The jump drive copies spreadsheet files. Follow the money, like Deep Throat said in *All The President's Men*.

You click on a folder labeled "Vacation pics" to see how much better a rich accountant lives. It's more porn, but by the lighting, it's amateurish and homemade. A picture on the wall shows the guy who must be the accountant shaking hands with an old lady and smiling as he holds a shiny gold plaque.

You glance back at the grainy video. That's Oswald tying up a crying blonde who looks awfully young. Hard to tell for sure and you can't bring yourself to keep watching. Oswald holds a leather cat-o-nine tails in one hand and his dick in the other. That little old lady with the plaque had no idea she was shaking the dick hand of a sadist. Shuddering, you click through his email, looking for clues and copying everything you can.

Check your watch. Move on.

RT THE DIVINE ASSASSIN PREFERS ARMANI @ASSASSINSPLAYBK

The place is spotless and smells like lemons, like the house is ready for one of those *Better Homes and Gardens* specials that makes a house look like an abandoned shrine. It's an atmosphere you associate with vacant people whose empty consumerism makes them obsessed with appearances. Obsessive cleanliness also makes you think of soulless serial killers trying to erase any trace of blood.

When you were a cop in the military walking into a case of a missing wife, the smell of bleach was a sure sign the grieving husband was actually "a person of interest." Technically speaking, you suppose you're a serial killer, too, but that doesn't count as long as you stay on the side of the angels. Mostly.

You explore the house, starting with the basement. If someone shows up looking for an intruder, you don't want to be the dumbass ninja stuck in the basement without multiple exits. There's a small storage area filled with old furniture. Most of the basement's square footage is a fancy games room with a sunken floor: full bar, huge sectional couches, a hot tub that's empty and dry, big flat screen and a pool table that makes you drool a little. It's a giant man cave.

Oswald is an asshole, but he still seems to have had more friends than you. However, this is the one place in the house with a coat of dust, so thick you might be the first person down here in months. Maybe Oswald was a big wheel, screwed up somehow and now Chill's client wants something on him for vengeance?

Hollywood is full of deals gone bad. Rifts, feuds and grudges aplenty result. You're going to have to find out. You don't like jobs where you don't know all there is to know about the client. Not knowing has gone badly in the past, but for a simple recon, you didn't want to press Chill. You trust him even if that means he doesn't trust you to spill everything up front. You can be patient.

There are three bedrooms, but two are empty to the bare walls. Oswald looks a youngish thirty, handsome and about your size, playing the field in kink. Those stark rooms tell a story: He's got no family who will ever visit. If he had a family, he's not tight with them now. Maybe his dad was eaten by sharks, too.

In the master bedroom, the bed is a king but Oswald sleeps alone. There are two nightstands, but the far one is empty. In the nightstand closest to the door, you discover a shiny .32 revolver in the drawer. You let him keep it, but in case Chill wants you to come back later, you empty the pistol and take all of Oswald's ammo.

You put the weapon back the way you found it and poke through more drawers. A wad of cash is rolled up in black socks so it stands to reason the house has no safe. You stuff the wad in your pocket and keep looking. Tie

16

pins, a dead watch, mismatched socks waiting for a lost mate. Nothing useful.

The walk-in closet is magnificent. It's more like another room than a closet. He's got rows and rows of shoes, each pair on a bamboo rack. Sadly, none of them are your size.

When you open the cedar cabinet to your left, you savor the smell of the wood. A line of linen dress shirts hangs ready and pressed, each in a plastic sheath from the dry cleaner. Each shirt is hung precisely two inches apart. The motorized tie rack proves he must be color blind, but the six sets of cufflinks are nice. The tie pins are gold and silver. You pocket the platinum cufflinks.

To your right, you find Oswald shares your taste in suits: all hail Armani. He's got suits like Batman has backup capes and cowls. You hope Chill will send you back here. You're going to want to steal more than you can carry. You sift through the suits. They're all black, except for a few pinstripes. You check the tags. They look a little long in the sleeve for you, but you can get that altered. It's Christmas in July.

A metallic scrape reaches your ear.

You pull the SIG as you spin, but you're alone. You wait. Hold that breath. Strain to the full range of your hearing.

Another, subtle scrape?

Yes. You're sure of the direction, but not of the source. You step toward the rack of suits, divide them, push them back. It's got to be a panic room. If Oswald is in there with a cell, you're already screwed. You can't let the cops take you alive. That leaves putting the muzzle under your chin and finding out what's next.

But it's not a panic room. There's a small lock at the

rear of the closet, just under the shelf. A gold key sits in the lock. Panic rooms, even disguised ones, lock from the inside. You turn the lock and, despite your effort to be quiet, the long dead bolt slides with a clunk. Expecting a shotgun blast to cut you in half, you spring back.

The desperate sob reaches out before the stench hits you. You know those smells: Meat gone bad and feces mix to make degradation. It's dark in there. "Hello?"

It's rough echolocation, but from the sound your voice makes, the room is bigger than you expected. You fish a small flashlight out of your pocket and peer in. You turn back to flick the switch in the walk-in closet and the fluorescents buzz and snap on with a low insectile hum.

You are unprepared for the utter horror that meets your eyes. The light spilling in through the secret door falls on a girl, tied to a wooden chair. Naked. Slumped. Dead. Half her head is shaved. The other half is a fall of red hair reaching past her broken shoulders. The hair runs to blood at the tips — her blood — like a paintbrush dipped in red. Her skin is a wretched map of criss-crossed welts and blossoms of old bruises.

The sob comes again. Your flashlight beam finds the beautiful Asian woman in the cage. Her red dress is ripped. One side of her face is a little swollen but otherwise? It's clear that Oswald hadn't started in on her yet.

You've known a lot of killers, but whoever did this? Worse. Monsters. Monsters erase humanity before they take the last breath and heartbeat.

This room a torture chamber like the one that trapped you in a Miami basement for three years. You want to throw up, but this is a crime scene so you hold

18

your burrito and sour coffee down.

You know better, but for some reason that denies reality, you try for a pulse at the woman's neck. You don't have to search for a pulse to confirm what you already know. The girl's skin is cold. You crouch at her feet. Her eyes stare back, the whites visible around the pupils.

Your stomach cramps and you curl up, fall to your knees and bow at her feet, as if in worship. The smell hits you harder and you can't keep your gorge down. You throw up the burrito and black coffee. You spew DNA all over the crime scene.

Soon, that won't matter. You aren't here to trap and relocate raccoons.

You just graduated to the role of exterminator. Again.

RT HAVE A FRIEND ON CALL WITH A LOAD OF GAS CANS. @ASSASSINSPLAYBK

When your stomach is empty, you straighten up and wipe your mouth on your sleeve. It's then that you realize the captive woman is staring and you're still holding your SIG in your hand, a little tighter than usual.

"I won't hurt you," you say, soft as you can. You drop the gun to your side and move a step toward her, but the light from the open door dims. The room is even darker and it takes you a second to work through what's going on.

"Jesus Diaz?" a gravelly voice asks.

You haven't heard that name, your real name, in months. *Uh-oh.*

He's large enough to almost fill the doorway. He has a barrel chest and a misshapen head too small for his body. Even in this light, pitted acne scars throw shadows across his face. He looks like a heavy sent over from Central Casting. Judging by the pictures in the living room and the video you saw, that's not Oswald. That's good news. The bad news is he knows your real name and you're sure the dark shape in his mitt is a pistol aimed your way.

"*Si?*"

"*Senor Diaz, quiero hablar con usted en privado.*"

You're nine feet apart in a very dark room. If you step closer to the light thrown through the secret door, you'll be going toward the light in the cosmic sense. You throw yourself behind the corpse in the chair and his gun barks twice. The woman in the cage screams.

You'd scream in terror, too, but you're busy. Flat on your belly behind the chair, the poor girl's body rocks above you. If you had stuffed your SIG back in its holster, the heavy would rush in and shoot you in the face at point blank range. You'd be shaking and fumbling for your weapon and dead. Instead, you're lining up your shot.

Your first two shots rip into his legs. You hoped for his knees, but a couple of chunks of meat and bone are sufficient.

He goes down on his back in the doorway with a grunt, half in the torture chamber and half out. "Esteban! Esteban!" He gets off another wild shot, but you can't miss your target now. You let the air out of that barrel chest and make his head more misshapen. When you click empty, you roll up and change mags.

The woman is still screaming. That's good because Esteban is coming and you need him distracted.

When you were a little boy in Cuba, you were in charge of babysitting your little brother, Rodolpho. You kicked a soccer ball back and forth, wandered the beach and begged for money from tourists. You were cute and Rodolpho was a painfully thin and sickly child so begging was the best use of your time.

Occasionally, you would entertain yourselves by spying

on your father as he cleaned the hotel pool. The game was to see how long you both could stalk him before he spotted you. When he was really little, Rodolpho proved to be too much of a giggler to be effective for long, but he got better at it under your stern tutelage.

Once, you told Rodolpho to sneak around to the stairs on the other side of the pool to spy on Marco Diaz. Meanwhile, you snuck up on your father, less than six feet away. Just as you were about to close the distance and lay a hand on your father's shoulder to surprise him, little Rodolpho pounded down the stairs on the other side of the pool. He might have weighed fifty pounds, but it was all in his heels. He slowed down the last few feet to go on tip-toe and peered around a potted palm. You and your father burst out laughing at your little brother's poor ninja skills.

You're reminded of your dead brother now as the heavy's ally, Esteban, pounds up the stairs in a blind rush screaming "Sergio! Sergio!" That is a tactical error.

You slip to the side of the door, your back flat against the wall. The dead guy stares up at you, blood still pumping from his wounds. With his hard looks, it's impossible to imagine he could ever have been anything else but the thug he was. With a face like that, you don't get to be a florist.

"Sergio!" Esteban arrives, breathing heavy. His gun hand pokes in the doorway first, arm straight.

"Don't! Don't!" The woman in the cage screams louder though you're sure she's huddled in a ball on the floor of her cage.

You hear the gunman's sharp intake of breath. That's surprise. He didn't expect to see the dead girl in the chair and he pauses to curse, *"Me cago en todo lo que se menea!"*

Before you learned English swear words, you translated the Spanish curses you knew from your father directly into English. When you tried to defy your captors, the worst thing you could think to say to them in broken English was, "I shit on everything that moves!" Hearing that expression again from the thug now makes you understand why the Bug Man and Tia Marta giggled a little before they reached for the hot iron to burn the defiance out of you.

"Diaz? A donde estas?" Esteban takes a half a step across the threshold. *"Te voy a matar!" I will kill you!*

That, you've heard many times.

On TV, the hero cracks the gunman's wrist with the butt of his pistol and easily disarms him. That would be good. You have a lot of questions that need answers. However, this ain't TV. Nothing goes that smooth and there are no second takes. The muzzle of the SIG grazes Esteban's left earlobe.

A single gunshot in a closed room sounds so loud, echoes of angry sound waves shimmer off the walls.

Esteban collapses atop Sergio. In the dim light, it looks like love.

RT JESUS PREFERS THE TERM TROUBLESHOOTER. #ASSASSINSPLAYBK

You don't want to leave the woman in the cage, but smart ninjas aren't soft ninjas. You step over the would-be assassins and quickly peek around the door, checking your angles. No one. Now that the gunfire is over, the house seems more still, as if everything, including the fish downstairs, are pausing to listen, too.

If Esteban had crept up the stairs and waited patiently for you to come out of the chamber of horrors, he could have easily shot you dead in the closet/shrine to Armani.

A window in the upstairs hallway to the street shows your car is where you left it, but a maroon Ford Shelby Mustang GT 500 sits behind it. The driver must have heard the shots and spotted you in the window. The engine roars to life and he peels out. You can't see the driver, but you're sure you'll meet soon. Next time, if he's smart, the guy in the Shelby will bring assassins who know better than to stand like silhouette targets in backlit doorways.

You didn't win today because you were especially smart. You're just smarter than the average hit man. That's usually enough. Hit man is a profession no different from plumbers and doctors and mechanics: there are few geniuses.

Before you turn on the torture chamber's light switch, you ask Oswald's prisoner, softly, not to scream. She does, anyway.

"*Sh. Sh.* You're out of danger."

She shakes her head and hugs herself. "No, I'm not."

She looks a little younger than you with skin that appears poreless. Her complexion is dark cream. She could be a model, which you suppose is why Oswald decided to trap her in his nightmare. You glance at your watch. When will Oswald return from work? You need back-up. Whatever schedule Chill had in his head, events have changed them.

There's a padlock on the woman's cage. Fortunately, the keys are on the floor a few feet away. That's a relief because shooting off the lock is another common trick in movies that requires special ammo. Try it in real life and the ricochet could kill you or her.

Before you open the lock, you look in her eyes. "Who's the girl in the chair?"

"Ginger Snap."

"So, a call girl?"

She nods. "Me, too."

"What's her real name?"

"Tabby Bernstein. She's from Indiana."

"Of course, she is. Where's your muscle?" Girls who look this good always have a driver who minds the girls when they go out on a job.

She shakes her head. "Ross said we'd make twice the money if we came to work on our day off, off the books, you know? He told us he could get us into movies. They all say that, but you keep hoping for a way out, you know?"

"I know." You ask her name.

"Sugar Cane."

"What's your real name?"

"Sugar Cane."

"C'mon."

"My parents hung out at Esalen a lot. That's what they named me. My sister's name is Candy."

"That's a great stripper name."

"My sister is a dental hygienist in Des Moines."

That tells you all you need to know about Sugar for now. "Excuse me, Sugar. I have a headache coming on."

Chill answers on the first ring. "Find anything?"

"Trouble."

"The cops show up?"

"Something about as bad. Emissaries from an ex best friend."

"What do you need?"

"Send Skunk to evac a vic to a hospital." You glance her way and she eyes you suspiciously. "Not the nearest hospital. I need time and I need Berb over here with gas cans. As many as he can get. Full."

"On the way." He clicks off.

"I'm not a 'vic'," Sugar says.

"You're crying. It's an easy mistake to make."

"I'm not a victim! I'm a casualty. Wrong place, wrong time. But her?" She nods to the dead naked woman. "He made me watch."

26

"Guy named Oswald, right?"

"Yes."

She knows his name, so he didn't plan for any prisoner in this room to survive captivity.

"Every terrible, filthy, disgusting thing he did to her, he made me watch. He told me I was next if I didn't cooperate. For, like, the second half of it? She didn't even make a sound. Cried from pain sometimes, but she didn't beg or plead. It was the bravest thing."

Before you can stop yourself, you say, "It wasn't bravery. It was surrender."

She's shocked for a moment and angry at you. "How would you know?"

You holster the SIG and pull up your shirt so she can see the crosses of scars across your belly. You've never willingly shown any woman your scars from Miami, but you need her to trust you. She needs to know you understand.

"I've been the person tied to the chair," you say. "Many times."

"You aren't a policeman," she says.

"I'm...something else."

"Don't call the police."

You glance at the bodies in the doorway. "Good advice."

"Not because of them."

"Oh?"

"The police are part of it. Prostitution, slavery, snuff films. There are police, high up. Oswald was saving me for the highest bidder."

This day was much better when you thought you were going to get some free suits out of an easy recon job.

"They're evil," Sugar says.

"How many in the ring?"

"Four that I've seen."

"It'll be okay," you say, feigning a self-assurance you don't feel. "I can fix this. Evil's my specialty." You pause. "Troubleshooting evil, I mean."

RT BETTER ASSASSINS ARE NOT TRACEABLE. #ASSASSINSPLAYBK

Chill hadn't told you the boys were on standby. They must have been because Skunk's red Crown Victoria rocks to a halt out front in a few minutes.

The crew calls him Skunk because he has a thick stripe of white through his black hair that reaches to the back of his head. Tall, 50ish, fit, ex-navy and the most experienced security guy in the company. He's reliable, but his moral inflexibility makes him the choice to spirit the girl to safety. He's not up for Dirty Tricks Department shenanigans.

After she steps over the dead men, Sugar looks back at you. "What will you do?"

"Something...fitting. Go with the nice man, now. He'll get you to an ER, okay?"

"Will I see you again?"

"Probably not."

"These men...they don't know mercy."

"I know the type. Thanks, Sugar. I'll take it from here. Why don't you disappear for a few days, in case I don't find them all right away."

You shoo her out and Skunk hustles her away. It's a relief to see her go. You let her see your scars. Before you spoke English well, you called them your "scares." You weren't wrong, either.

While you wait for Berb to bring the gas cans, you search pockets. Esteban carried an ugly Smith & Wesson and a pack of Nicorette gum.

"Good news!" you announce to the half of Esteban's head that's still together. "You've quit smoking, scumbag. Lung cancer is a tough way to die. You're welcome. *Hombres necios…*"

Sergio had a Springfield Armory XD-S.45, good for concealment but comically small in his huge ham of a fist. Sergio carried enough extra mags to suggest he was either a terrible shot, a hoarder or he was expecting a shoot out with dozens of gunmen.

Neither would-be assassin carries a wallet, ID or even keys. Even the tags are ripped out of their sports jackets. They got everything right except the "deadly" part of ninja assassin.

All you really know is they spoke Spanish and they wanted to get information out of you before killing you. Most important, they knew your real name. In California, you're Dr. J.D. Fix. No one besides ex-girlfriends, New York's Spanish Mob, the FBI, Homeland Security, Chill, Sgt. Billy — and now Sugar — know your real name. The first four might shoot you on sight. The last three, you have to trust.

You've never met these guys, of course. They're undoubtedly locals working for The Machine. New York's Spanish Mob knows your name and they have not forgotten what you did to them.

30

You glance at your watch. There's no point calling Berb. He's coming as fast as he can and the timing will be tight. You need the gas cans before Oswald comes home. Berb doesn't want to take part in what you're about to do any more than Skunk, but he'll show with the accelerant.

In the torture chamber, you notice something disturbing and possibly useful. In the corner sits a tripod. There's no camera, but someone recorded what went on in this room. You hope you never have to see that recording.

Deep breath.

You step to the girl in the chair. She stares at you. That's another thing TV and movies get wrong. You can try to close the eyes of the dead, but it doesn't work. They keep staring back, asking why. Or maybe, "Is that all there is?"

A large mattress with no box spring or bed frame sits on the floor. There's a single soiled sheet that will have to serve as the girl's shroud. You cut her bonds with your switchblade and catch her before she slips from the chair. Despite the blood, shit and piss, you cradle her to your chest, carry her, and lower her to the mattress gently. You wrap her in the sheet slowly, with reverence.

"I'm so sorry this happened to you. Don't be embarrassed," you say. "You did nothing wrong. I promise they won't do it again. I'll make sure they never hurt anyone again. I'll make sure they're sorry they did this."

The girl couldn't have been older than eighteen.

You whisper the only prayer you really believe: "They don't have it in them to feel for other people. There's something wrong with their brains. Don't worry, though. I'll make sure they feel regret. They have no empathy, but they've got nerves for pain, just like everybody else. I'll make them find regret, somewhere deep down in the bone. I promise, over your dead body. Amen."

You finish crying before Berb arrives.

RT HIT MEN IN THE KNOW UNDERSTAND WHAT EXOCULATE MEANS. @ASSASSINSPLAYBK

When Ross Oswald III pulls up to his house in his BMW, you wonder what he's thinking about. Do monsters so compartmentalize their lives that they're pretty much like everyone else when at work? Does he really focus on his spreadsheets, or is the background music playing in his mind a constant pounding drum: rape, murder, destroy, rape, murder, destroy?

You could ask him, but you have more pressing issues on your mind. You have to take him down before the smell of gas everywhere tips him that something is amiss. You're also concerned how many times you can use the stun gun without killing him. You don't want to be premature on that, but you'll just have to experiment.

When he opens the front door, briefcase in hand, you greet him with a cheery, "Science can be fun!" Two barbed darts deliver lightning to his face.

You zap him five times before he rolls around enough to tangle himself in the wires. Tetany through his muscles makes his hands into claws. His throat and face strain and his eyes goggle up at you, bewildered. Through the miracle of electricity, he looks more like the monster he really is beneath the nice suits.

"Good evening, Oswald. I notice in all your correspondence, nobody seems to call you Oz. Oswald sucks but Oz is a cool name. How come no one calls you Oz?"

After a while, through tears and gasping for breath he manages, "What?"

"We're all here to learn, pal." You zap him again. "Try to focus, Oz. I was talking about your name and waiting for you to give me the slightest reason to pull this trigger again. Unfair of me, I know, but we both know you don't have a right to ask for what's fair. If I run out of juice in this stun gun — I think the limit on this battery charge is twenty-five electrocutions — I'll have to switch to low-tech tactics. Did you know that there's a two percent chance with every zap that you could experience the agony of testicular torsion? Usually when I want testicular torsion, I have to go old school and do it manually, but through the miracle of technology — "

Zaaaaaap!

Crying. Drooling. It looks like a seizure, but he's fully awake, conscious of every amp and volt shooting through his body, racking him with spasms. When you took your training as a Military Policeman, they called the stun guns "conducted energy weapons." That sounded pretty fancy and futuristic for what they are.

Your instructor, Sgt. "The Devil" Devin, would call the agony Oswald is now suffering "temporary neuromuscular disruption." When you pull the trigger and let the current ride, he is your puppet. The girl in the chair was no doubt his puppet, too. You wonder if she's watching. You'd like to think so.

"Come to think of it, given what you are, maybe I should have shot you in the nuts instead of the face. Or I could use your own cattle prod on you. I found it up in that secret room. That would be justice, wouldn't it, Oz?"

His eyes are huge with fear and his pupils are pinpricks. He nods minutely.

"That's the right answer."

He nods harder, eager to please.

You zap him again, the electric gun ticking as it delivers the volts. "Nobody likes a suck up, Oz."

RT FOR INTERROGATION, PREPARE DONNY OSMOND PATTER. @ASSASSINSPLAYBK

You give Oswald some time to recover and let his fear grow. "You a Donny and Marie fan, Oz? Don't answer that. *Everybody's* an Osmond fan, though I'm a little higher on Donny than Marie. She's sweet, but he did that really funny video with Weird Al called *White & Nerdy* a few years ago. You see it? Hilarious. I'd tell you to YouTube that shit, but you don't have that kind of time."

He studies you, looking for an angle. If he knew about your childhood in Miami, he'd rediscover a childhood prayer instead of trying for a way out.

"If they're old enough, everyone thinks of Donny in his early purple socks and *Puppy Love* days. They forget about his stab at a comeback. He made a really good song and kind of a sexy video. That was toward the end of music videos being relevant. Do you remember that? He sang a song called *Soldier of Love*. Pretty catchy. I liked it so I ended up getting hooked on the stuff from when he was young. Movies and happy music...such beautiful escapes.

If you had it here, I'd play *Soldier of Love* for you. When I go, I'd be okay with that as the soundtrack for my death scene. How about you? What music would you like to play you off the stage?"

"I can give you money."

"I've been upstairs, Oz. You don't have that level of moolah."

"I could! I could get it to you! Lots of money!"

He shuts up when you raise the stun gun. "After what I saw, you'd need more money than the Sultan of Brunei for me to pause just for two seconds. You'd need more money than God, Oz. You'd need Pope-level money for me to give you another night on earth. Read me?"

When he nods you lower the stun gun, sit down and get comfortable. "Where was I before you interrupted?"

"You...you...were talking about Donny Osmond."

"Right! Great performer. Caught him and Marie in Vegas on my trip out here. Good show, but weird show. She makes surprisingly bawdy jokes. She's still cute. And you know what, thinking about you and Donny...it got me thinking about redemption. I was thinking about how we're all looking for redemption. We all want to stay on top or make a comeback. We all want to be right and we all want to be loved. Sometimes we have to change our names and, what would an uber-corporate wage ape like you call it? Rebranding!"

He's nodding, which makes you want to zap him again, but if he has a stroke, he'll be much less coherent.

"Anyway, years back, when *Soldier of Love* came out, some VJ suggested that Donny reinvent himself. She said he should change his name to Oz or maybe it was *The* Oz. Or maybe The Great and Powerful Oz. He hasn't aged a bit, you know. He's one of those guys like Rob Lowe. Makes you wonder if they have a deal with the devil. Have you got a deal with the devil, Oz? You seem pretty well set up here, rich…lots of pricey fish…secret torture chamber and all. I'm wondering who the devil is? Can you tell me? Who is the devil behind you?"

"What do you want to know?"

"Names."

"Which ones?"

"All of them."

"You don't know these people."

"You don't understand me yet, Oz. Think of me as your opposite number. I'm a lot like you. You're bent wrong. I'm bent right. Like Jimmy Cagney said in *The Strawberry Blonde*, 'That's the kind of hairpin I am.' You know that movie? 1941. Kinda sappy, but it's still Cagney."

"They'll kill me."

"You *know* you're dead already."

"Then what's in it for me if I cooperate?"

You eye the stun gun and set it down on the floor as you pull out the switchblade. His gaze is fixed on the knife. Strangely, from your experience with situations like this, a blade scares guys much more than a handgun, at least until they get shot. It's time to pull back and use a little finesse.

"I knew somebody like you when I was a kid, Oswald. She taught me how to speak English like an American, among other things. She thought having a large vocabulary was important. For instance," you show him your shiny blade, "do you know what 'exoculate' means? I'll give you a clue. It has to do with your eyes."

Oswald begins to weep. "C'mon, man! Give me

38

something here!"

"I'll give you a choice of how you die. I promise you that. You *will* have a choice."

"That's not much of a deal."

"This isn't a negotiation. With those darts in your face, I might make you dance all night. Or I could use this knife and make you my puppet the old-fashioned way and shove it up your ass. Take the deal and spill everything, or I promise you, we'll go through my full vocabulary, E - Z. We'll start with 'exoculate.'"

RT JESUS & ANDREW DICE CLAY DRIVE A FORD FAIRLANE @ASSASSINSPLAYBK

His face is bloody from where you ripped out the darts. Oswald's still begging you to shoot him as he climbs on the chair.

You aim the SIG at his crotch. "If I shoot you, it'll be in the left testicle. It'll hurt, but you'll still end up in that tank." You raise the Zippo. "Get in there."

Oswald tumbles into the big aquarium, frightening clouds of yellow tangs. Displaced water gushes over the floor. His head pops up and he sputters. "Call the cops! I'll confess everything! I'll go to prison!"

"And let you get repeatedly beaten, tortured and raped? That would be wrong, Oz. I don't want to sink to your level. That would be evil and I'm just bad. In fact, I'll prove to you I'm not the monster you are."

You raise the stereo remote and click play. Oswald's Bose sound system blasts out *Hard Knock Life* by Jay-Z. It's not *Soldier of Love*, but it's not bad at all. The song is far too fine for the thing in the aquarium that's been impersonating a human being.

You step to the front door and toss the Zippo behind you. The flame's blossom is a beautiful rush, taking over the room, climbing walls and circling the fish tank.

"Shoot me! Shoot me, you son of a bitch! You said I had a choice! Shoot me! You said I had a choice!"

Over the roar of the inferno chewing through the house, a rhyme occurs to you. "Maybe you'll boil! Maybe you'll fry! Drown or broil, prepare to die!"

Oswald looks back at you uncomprehending. "*What?*"

Some people just don't appreciate rap.

"I never said I'd shoot you, Oz! Your choice is drown or burn! It's up to you!"

"You're so sure what's wrong with me!" he sputters. "What's wrong with *you?*"

"Gandhi said, 'Be the change you want to see in the world!' That's what I'm doing!" You turn from the wall of heat, leaving him to hell.

But you are more than a little haunted by his question. What is wrong with you? The real answers? Trauma, drama and a tragic lack of choices, you suppose. But who cares? Everybody has an opinion on how people should be, but you are what you are. You tell the night, "I am a special snowflake. I love me."

You walk back to the Fairlane and climb in, watching the orange light spread from window to window. Smoke pours out the front door. You left a trail of gasoline to a couple of gas cans in the torture room. It doesn't take long for the spreading flames to find that fuse and race into the torture chamber.

When the explosion hits, the concussion is bigger than expected. Oswald's next-door neighbors' car alarms begin

41

to blare and people come out of their homes, all reaching for their cell phones at once, pointing and yelling to each other. Despite all the noise, Oswald's screams penetrate the din.

You thought it was possible the fire could suck up all his oxygen. Maybe he'd drown or maybe, since he was all wet anyway, he'd try to make a run for it through the field of flame. In the end, it's the roof collapsing that cuts his last scream short.

Satisfactory.

You've destroyed *two* very nice houses and one crappy one in your career as the divine assassin. Some people might begin to think something is seriously wrong with you. However, you tell yourself nothing is a habit until you do it consistently for much longer. Three weeks straight, the productivity experts say. Yes, burning down a house each day for three straight weeks? *That* would be excessive. You do feel bad about the fish. There wasn't time to save them.

Strangely, there's still power in the flaming ruins. The roof collapse didn't get the stereo yet. You can still just catch the little kids singing the chorus to *Hard Knock Life*.

The Fairlane's engine cranks to a soothing rumble that drowns out the music. The shouts of excited neighbors are all that's left now. You pull away as sparks fly and embers drift into an orange sky toward the white gaze of a ripe moon.

You gave up on God when Tia Marta beat that hope out of you, but, figuring it can't hurt, you offer a prayer for the girl's eternal rest as she cremates.

Sirens reach through the night to announce that the firefighters are on their way. You have some names and

42

more fires to put out. You slowly motor away from what was supposed to be a simple recon mission.

The two would-be assassins don't get any prayers from you. However, you do thank Ross Oswald III for all the fine Armani suits and silk shirts stuffed in the trunk.

RT CALIFORNIA WOMEN ARE WORTH THE EARTHQUAKES. @ASSASSINSPLAYBK

Whenever you get to a new town, you act like a tourist. You take the bus tours, fitting in easily with all the slack-jawed rubes. Some tours are better than others but they hit most of the same hot spots: the Chinese Theater, Hollywood Boulevard, The Hollywood Bowl, Universal CityWalk and the Hollywood Sign. The best tour went through the Hills, pointing out various celebrity homes.

You took a double decker bus with the same tour guide twice because he was so entertaining and appeared so knowledgeable. "That one belongs to director Kevin Smith! This beautiful house belongs to comedian Joe Rogan! That one belongs to Molly Ringwald from *The Breakfast Club* and various John Hughes' movies!"

On the second tour, the guide didn't assign the same mansion to the same star twice. Kevin Smith's house was now Ben Stiller's place. Rogan's compound became Bill Maher's. That's so Hollywood. You laughed until you could hardly breathe. Even hairpins like you who have already been duped plenty. You've played deception games of your own, too, but anyone can be conned. It's often surprisingly easy.

In the neighborhoods reserved for celebrities and the idle rich, you don't actually see the really fabulous houses. The really nice mansions, like Johnny Depp's place — or at least the place you *think* belongs to Johnny Depp — is far behind high hedges concealing razor wire. Bus tours allow the rubes to admire the smaller mansions you can see from the road. These are probably the houses that belong to the armies of lawyers and accountants who work for celebrities and the idle rich. "Accountants of the Idle Rich." That would be a great name for a band.

You drive aimlessly, using the time to think. You got Sgt. Billy to buy you the Ford Fairlane at a police auction. The engine needs tuning, but as you drive with the windows rolled down and the wind in your hair, the uneven rumble under the drum of the hood is soothing.

You rarely drove in New York. California is for driving. You've been up and down the coast many times to visit Hearst Castle, The Mystery House and to ride the streetcars in San Francisco. The best driving is out of the city. L.A.'s traffic is so congested and slow, it actually makes the city feel much bigger than it already is. Just a few miles as the crow flies can take at least an hour, picking your way through the city's sprawl and bumper-to-bumper traffic. Miles are not covered well within the city. Time is wasted.

One weekend, with no work from Chill to hold you, you drove to San Jose and sang along with Dionne Warwick as the CD played *Do You Know the Way to San Jose?* You sang it over and over until Sgt. Billy reached up from the back seat, ejected the CD and threw it out of the car window. He called you a little kid that day. He hasn't stopped. That makes you happy, like you've got a father again (but new and improved from the murderous Marco).

You should be dead, or at least pacing in a tiny concrete cell, so you relish everything California has to offer: a better father, a boss who's a friend and scenery accented with palm trees and beautiful women. Tens are everywhere (and even the fives dress like tens).

Beautiful women are to California what windmills are to Holland: they define the landscape. The women move alone and in groups, heads up and always going somewhere with a confident stride. Women in New York have a similar stride, but always look harried, hurrying on like they're perpetually late for an appointment.

California women move with equal purposefulness, but they seem assured that even if they're late, they're worth the wait. They are powered by the sun and always sure the future is bright. California during the day is all smiles and summer dresses. The view is worth the earthquakes.

By the time you find yourself in Pompano Beach, you're ready to work out your next move. Around Progresso Village, you park when you find a Wifi connection that's not locked up. On any street, there are still people who do not password protect their modems, much to the delight of sex offenders looking for untraceable downloads. And avengers like you.

You text Chill and he texts back right away. "Smooth?"

"Shiny."

"News?"

"Oswald did *not* act alone."

You touch the icon for Evernote and send him the

names. Four targets. Then you tell Chill you really need to know who the client is and chat with him.

It's not a him. It's a her and it's a name everyone knows: Legs Gabrielle.

He sends you a photo. You've seen the starlet nearly naked in Esquire in the "Women We Love" photo shoot. Another pic of Legs isn't necessary, though you do appreciate it.

Chill sends another pic. However, this one is not Legs Gabrielle. It's a thick-necked bruiser, all steroid jaw and dead eyes under a blonde brush cut. The insolent slash of his mouth makes his look more Aryan Nations than ex-military.

You go cold when you see Chill's next text. It reads: *Detective* Hank Reles. LAPD. 6'4, and trouble. Claims to be Ex Spec Ops for the navy. He's the client's stalker."

Shit. He's one of the names you squeezed out of Oswald.

Chill tells you where to find her. He's on his way soon.

It seems your night is far from over. You smell like gasoline, so you change in a gas station, wash up as best you can and ditch your ruined clothes in a dumpster eight blocks away before turning around.

Time to catch a rising star, but how are you going to kill the devil without drawing all of hell's heat?

RT DO THE TIME? YOU GET TO DO THE CRIME @ASSASSINSPLAYBK

Sal's Comedy Hole on Melrose. You find a place to park a couple of blocks away and head in. You've been here before. It's a fun, funky place with no drink minimum and a different atmosphere than most comedy clubs. There are couches, for one thing. It reminds you of a couple of cozy clubs back in New York.

When you walk in, you don't have to scan the crowd for Legs. She's already onstage doing a set. A movie star doesn't have to do stand-up anymore. However, you've seen Conan and Kimmel interview her. It doesn't matter how beautiful she is or how many movies she's in. Legs Gabrielle was funny first and loves the work.

The crowd laughs in all the right places. The way she paces the stage, a panther in a cage, reminds you of Chris Rock's early days. Most female comics stand still and are conversational. Legs is balls out aggressive, daring the audience not to laugh.

You scan the crowd for Reles. Given his size, he'll be hard to miss. You slip to the side so you can watch Legs, the crowd, the front door and the exits.

"Where my stoners at?" Legs Gabrielle scans the crowd. "It's okay! You can tell me! It's just between us!"

One guy half-way back raises a hand.

"What's your name, sweetie?"

"Paul."

"That's nice. What's your last name?"

"Um…Burnell."

She pounces. "Awesome. Paul Burnell! Now where are my law enforcement officers? Gotta be at least one in the crowd! You better have your card for that weed, Paul, or you're headed to jail!"

No one raises a hand, but she slips into her saver for the joke. "That's cool. That's cool. The cops are undercover tonight. There's an easy way to spot 'em, though. Narcs can't help themselves. Any hecklers show up? We'll know, *that's* a narc. Humor narc, weed narc. Same thing. They see somebody else having fun and they gotta smack that right down! That or the narc will show himself by giving my new friend Paul here a cavity search out front of the club later!"

The laughter barely dies down when she hits again. "Don't be confused. If Paul is getting a cavity search in the men's room between sets, that's not necessarily a narc. That could just be a friend of Paul's, so don't be hatin'!"

The crowd is really going with it, but she manages to top herself. "I was just up in Canada and the cops up there are cool about weed. Besides, if the guy's got a gun, you *want* him to chillax and chillaze with some weed. Up there? They give you a stern talking to, steal your weed and go smoke it right in front of you on their horse. Maybe even give the horse a puff just to piss you off.

That's not bad. Bad is, in most states? They take away your house, your car, your job, your life, your kids and toss your ass in prison for years for the victimless crime of talking stupid while you look up at the stars!"

You're scanning the room for a monster, but she's got you chuckling a little bit.

"Which would you rather? Have a trip to the principal's office or have everything taken away? Stern talking to or have sex in a very small room next to a toilet with a guy named Mary, like our poor stoner friend, Paul Burnell, here? I'll take that trip to the principal's office. Go ahead, Mr. Mountie! Get your horse high and taunt me with my own stash! I'll take it! It's better than having prison sex with Paul!"

The room erupts and Burnell stands, puts both hands in the air and bows to Legs like he's worshipping her.

"...just kidding, Paul! Give me a call when you get some good weed, baby! I prefer the AK Kush or BC Bud, cool?"

Her voice is still sweet, but her pace is machine gun fast and she has the crowd in her fist. "Of course, weed is a luxury. It's not weed we really want. You know what women want, fellas? I'm sorry to tell you, size does matter. When we pull you into bed, we want a big...strong... meaty...*jaw!* No! You don't get to breathe until I say you can breathe. You get to breathe, maybe, when I'm done! Now get in there and enjoy dessert first if you even *hope* you're going to have a shot at the main course!"

The audience roars, even the few who look disapproving and embarrassed. Legs calls out a woman who's frowning and shaking her head but laughing despite herself.

"Oh, no, bitch, you can't have it both ways. You don't

get to laugh first and then call my act dirty! You laughed. We saw you. You can't take it back. And later tonight, when you take your man home, you'll be *telling* him that joke over and over. Hell, you'll be acting it out. It's just a joke, baby! Don't smother him!"

You don't know how long she's been up there, but she only waits a moment before the next line of attack.

"And fellas, if you're going to watch that nasty porn, take it as an instructional video. You will be graded on this oral exam if you ever expect to test me on the supplementary anal."

The room goes nuts again and when that wave of laughter subsides, Legs goes into crowd work, setting up the next punch. "What about it, ladies? When you catch your man watching porn, is that cheating?"

A couple of women near the front answer yes. Legs zeroes in on the closest couple. "Do you know this man?"

"That's my husband."

"I was hoping since you have your hand in his crotch," — the woman jumps in her seat, raises both hands and laughs — "but I didn't want to assume. I thought maybe you're just friendly. What's your name, sweetie?"

"Challa," the woman answers, loud and proud.

"And your man's name?"

"Dave!" Dave, a wimpy-looking dude in a yellow sweater vest, looks like he might crawl under his chair to escape. His cheeks flush crimson.

"Dave, have you been on those websites? Did you forget to clear out your browser's history, you poor dumb bastard?"

To his credit, the guy smiles, nodding. The crowd cheers his embarrassment and he tries to wave Legs

Gabrielle off, begging for mercy. He might as well have been waving a slab of red meat at a tiger.

"Dave, Challa is very angry with you. I can tell. She's calling you out in front of all these people, man! She's telling you very clearly that pornography is cheating!"

A basso rumble of discontent reaches her from the back of the crowd and Legs wheels on them. "Some of your boys are thinking they should come to your defense, Dave, but those guys are either single or they're sitting beside their date right now and pretending they don't even know what porn is! They make it all in Pasadena, fellas! You trying to tell me you've never heard of youporn? Or xhamster.com? Dave knows those sites and," she points to another victim, "and this guy here is taking notes so he won't forget the name of that website when he gets home! You can tell he's alone. He's one of those small-jawed guys!"

Legs points at another man standing off to the side at the front and you're surprised to find it's Berb, her bodyguard for the evening. As soon as he left you, he must have reported for his babysitting shift.

"See the jaw on this guy?" Legs says. "Dude's got a jaw like a steam shovel." She mimes holding a phone, winks and smiles and mouths, "Call me."

People are rocking in their seats with laughter. It's not just laughter, though. It's energy that bounces off the walls and moves through the crowd, amping everyone up.

"So guys, here's the real deal. Dave, Challa feels that porn is cheating so you have to stop that shit. I'm not saying I agree. I'm saying that's your lady's policy so now it's your policy. Pornography is cheating! So, Dave. You know what you gotta do now, right? You gotta delete those nasty websites, tune up your jaw muscles — chew a lot of gum — and head on over to some nasty *dating* websites. Hook me up *now* dammit! dot com…Just blow me quick cuz I don't want to do any of the work…dot org…I need a guy with a steam shovel jaw…dot net. Get out and find yourself a *real* woman, Dave! You know why? Because Challa *already* thinks you're a cheater! If you're going to do the time, Dave, you get to do the *crime*!"

Women scream and men howl with laughter and before that can die down, Legs leaves the stage on a high note, pausing to give a dainty curtsy, blowing kisses as she exits.

RT SECURITY FIRMS HAVE BODYGUARDS. YOU'RE AN ATTACK DOG. @ASSASSINSPLAYBK

Berb spots you and waves you over. He only knows you by one name. "Fix! Chill told me you're getting called in on this one."

He doesn't ask about the gas cans. Berb is a professional so he's got instant amnesia. If you brought up the evening's earlier adventures, he'd look at you like a bulldog looks at a ceiling fan, bewildered maybe, but not curious.

Not curious is good. He's a bodyguard. You're something else Hollywood security firms never speak of. He plays defense. You play offense. Sometimes you wish you had his job.

You tell Berb you're here to keep an eye out for the same threat he is: Reles.

"You met Legs, yet?"

"Uh-uh. How long you been babysitting?"

"For a month at least. Me, Skunk and the new Samoan. It's been one on one until a couple of days ago. Then Chill put us all on her. Threat's up, but I don't know the details why."

"I think I know why. What's she like?"

"She's nice," Berb says. "Unlike some people in her profession, she's not always on, so she's almost like a regular human when she isn't in front of a crowd."

"Almost?"

"Well, look at her. Gorgeous, funny, smart, rich and getting richer. The whole package."

"I'll be glad to see the client and congratulate her on a great set. She destroyed."

"No time. We're on the move in a second. You'll have lots of chances to talk, though," Berb adds. "We're headed back to Legs' place right away. I already put the call in to Chill — he's still on his way — but we need you, too. We're calling in reinforcements."

"What's up?"

Berb can't be older than twenty-five, but his face is heavy and as serious as an old man. "A security nightmare. I like Miss Gabrielle a lot, but she's throwing an impromptu party. She must think she's out of danger because she's not listening to me at all, man."

"Cabin fever?"

He nods. "They all get it eventually. Chill called her and she was suddenly acting like a princess sick of being locked in the tower. I get it. Everybody gets tired of being surrounded by babysitters."

Chill must have told her he had his special ops guy (i.e. you) on the case. "Her relaxation of vigilance and celebration is premature."

"That's okay. We'll stay frosty. Skunk's already got the egress covered and the Samoan's by the car watching for stage door Johnnies. Next stop: Legs Gabrielle's house."

He flashes you the address from his phone.

It will be nice to hang out in a mansion with no hidden horrors in secret bloody rooms. Not blowing up a mansion will also be a positive change of pace.

Berb tells you what he knows. Chill proposed that the easiest way to deal with Detective Reles was to get Legs out of town. However, she's got auditions to attend and stand-up gigs to do. All her work is in Los Angeles so she can't give her stalker a cooling off period.

She wants to live her life, do her work and live her dream unharassed. That's reasonable. You understand. However, once Reles finds out one of his torture ring buddies is dead, things could get hot. In your mind, it's a torture ring. You refuse to think of what happened to that poor girl as sex.

You're on your way out when you spot Reles near the door. He's on his way out, too. He must have been pressed against the back wall in the shadows behind a pillar. He's cagey. You need to know more but you can't come straight at the guy. You know Reles is dangerous because you had to zap Oswald until the stun gun's battery drained. Then you had to use old school, manual techniques to get the predator's name. Oswald gave up Reles last.

Reles is the scariest kind of crazy. He's got a badge.

Your power and authority comes from the weight of Ginger's dead gaze. Her name in the real world was Tabby. Tabitha. It was a beautiful name for a girl who didn't get a chance to pull herself out of Hollywood's underground.

Tonight, it's time for another recon mission. In the best case scenario, Reles and his circle of monsters disappear. Then you'll disappear, too, preferably to another country, at least for a while.

How you're going to manage all that? You have no idea.

You think of Ginger's dead gaze again. All you do know is, tonight? Vengeance wears Armani.

RT WHEN CONFRONTING EVIL, LOOK FRIENDLY (AT FIRST.) @ASSASSINSPLAYBK

You don't have to follow him far. Reles crosses the street to a coffee shop, orders a drink and sits on the tiny outdoor patio. When you cross the street, he appears to stare at you. Then you realize he looks at everyone that way, mad at the world. He looks like a cannibal who hasn't eaten in days and has a new bottle of barbecue sauce at the ready.

Reles is one of those big, sandy-haired California dudes who looks like he spends all his spare time pumping iron and trying to make his neck bigger. His shoulders are so yoked, he looks out of place in the cafe's patio lawn chair, like an adult in a child's plastic chair.

Slap on your happiest smile. As Jack Lemmon used to say before the camera rolled, "It's magic time!" You throw Reles a flirty wink as you pass him. His jaw tightens and he looks away.

The woman in front of you in line has a complex order and a problem with her credit card. You take the opportunity to call Chill on your throwaway and tell him where you are.

"What's your plan?"

"I have no idea, so…improv. I'll take his temperature."

"Don't use the rectal thermometer until you've got a solid plan, Jesus."

"Roger that."

"Go full drama," Chill suggests. "From what Legs tells me, he thinks of himself as a tough guy."

"He has the look that tells me that's real."

"Then shake him up with your musical theater schtick."

"It's not a schtick. It's a character."

"Sure, sure, Pacino. Just get him off balance and come up with a plan. The fact that he's a cop…it's complicated."

"Yes, mother."

The clog in the artery to the barista is finally clear. Everyone has a story, so for practice you take what you think is a pretty good guess about the young woman behind the counter. The barista speaks to the customers in a monotone that suggests she's on some kind of downer but she enunciates each word, so maybe she has a mild case of Aspergers. She's about twenty-three and thin with that sinewy, unhealthy look Yoga vegans get when they do too many of the wrong drugs. She has a hard look around her mouth and her eyes are squinty, as if she's perpetually looking at the world through smoke.

Slathered in tattoos of mythical animals and awash in retail boredom, you spot what you think is phoenix doing battle with a gryphon. The blue tattoos — not yet completed so she's probably saving up for color — spread up from her push-up bra cleavage to her throat.

She wears a name tag that reads: Raven. Her

grandparents probably went to Berkeley and her parents are stoners but she's working a Starbucks because she's living with some dude studying neo-fascism AKA law school at UCLA.

"Darling!" you burst. "I am *so* in need of a decaf venti latte with a dusting of cinnamon, I can't tell you!" You might have overshot the runway. Your first attempt sounds more like Truman Capote on helium, so you try to dial it back when you say, "Thanks, sweetie. Love the dragon eating the gryphon. Very neo-D&D revivification."

Raven gives you a plastic smile that tells you to drop dead. Despite the traffic, Reles must have heard you out on the patio so there's no way he'll think you're any danger to him. Macho guys like Reles always assume gay guys are no threat, even though that's obviously stupid. Chill is gay and he could pound just about anybody to dust. You happen to know he has on several occasions.

You get your drink, swish out to the patio and slide into a seat at the little table next to Reles. The key to meeting people is not to wait and let the tension build where it's obvious you're speaking out of loneliness as a last resort. To make this play work, you have to channel crazy Aunt Sadie. Everybody knows a crazy Aunt Sadie who can't shut up for a minute as long as she's conscious.

"Hello! Do you know who I just saw in that club across the street?"

Reles turns his head slowly and looks you up and down, assessing. When you wink and smile again, taking his threat assessment as a sexy invitation, his upper lip curls. Misinterpreting a threat as a come-on is the easiest way to throw off a threat assessment.

"Not interested."

"Oh, really? Do you know who Legs Gabrielle is?"

His head snaps around again. "What about her?"

"She's a dolly. Just a dolly."

"Yeah, she is." At the corner of his mouth, he allows a hint of a grudging smile.

"I talked to her and you know what? She talked to me! It was like the television just came alive!"

"What name do you go by, muchacho?"

Like dialogue from an old Western, you think. "Delgado, but you can call me Armando. Everybody does. And what's your name, kind sir?"

"Hank," he says, taking another sip of his coffee. "What did Legs say?"

"Oh, my God, yes. I have a friend who works backstage. I spoke to Legs Gabrielle. And you know what's better? She couldn't have been sweeter."

"What'd she say?" He's intrigued and impatient.

"I asked her what her perfume was because it was beautiful. It smelled like roses."

"Armando," Reles says. "I didn't ask what you said. I asked what she said."

Typical cop mentality: entitled. You probably sounded the same when you first became a Military Policeman. A lot of guys get badge-heavy and stay badge-heavy. Give anybody a special hat and power over others and they will abuse that power. Studies prove it. Given how you held Oswald's life in your hand tonight and squeezed, you don't need to google a scientific study. You know it personally. Subtract the sex crimes and maybe you aren't so different from Reles.

When you pick up your drink for another sip, your hand shakes. You were supposed to rattle him. Instead, he's shaking you.

RT CHILDREN ARE HOLY TO THE DIVINE ASSASSIN @ASSASSINSPLAYBK

"Hello?"

There's something familiar about Reles. Something about him makes you want to wipe the smug off his face with a power sander.

You take another swig of coffee to give yourself time and think about what to say next. Just because you're playing a gay guy doesn't mean you have to play the role without dignity. "Bitch, please, I'm getting to that. I asked her about her perfume and she said she only wears lavender."

An ex of yours wore that scent. The lovely Lily. To this day, the scent of lavender still stirs happy memories, way back last summer, before the New York mob wanted you punished, then dead. Somewhere out there, another guy much like you is no doubt hunting you. It's like it's always rabbit season and your only hope is to lose yourself in the city's warren of dives. You're always hiding in a hole and, behind the scenes of every day life, there are so many hunters.

"Miss Gabrielle said she got the perfume on her last trip to Canada," you add. "They were shooting her latest film. Something awful. Another horror movie."

"I love her horror movies."

"That's not my cup of pee, Hank, but to each his own. I prefer her stand-up. I saw a clip of her work...the Montreal Comedy Festival, I think it was. Very funny. Very racy, as I recall."

"Yeah. I've heard all her stuff." His gaze never leaves the entrance to the comedy club. "She's a dirty bitch. I'd love to see her on her knees with clothespins on her nipples."

You drop out of character for a second and just say, "Shit, man."

"She's a buffet." Reles looks at you for the first time in several minutes and you see something in his eyes you recognize. "With lots of cinnamon! I can't tell you!" he adds, mocking you.

You know that face. His is the confidence of a wolf among sheep. The woman and man who kidnapped you, Tia Marta and the Bug Man, had the same dead eyes.

LAPD's psychologist must have been asleep the day they let this guy in the door. A lot of candidates fail those tests simply because they answer the crucial question wrong. When asked why they want to be cops, the correct answer is, "To serve and protect." Blather a few banalities about respect, love of order and being a peace officer and you're in.

Most monsters are so dumb, they think the correct answer is, "To enforce the law and finally get the respect I deserve." Then they're out the door and wondering why they can't ever be police officers. Then they go into low level security jobs or they become deputies in remote Texas towns shaking down brown people and tourists. Or the rejects get elected governor of Texas. They go anywhere they can wield power unchecked. Detective Hank Reles has the look of a guy who should definitely *not* be in authority.

That look in his eyes…you've caught that look in mirrors sometimes. You tell yourself again that you're nothing like this asshole. You're just a guy who finds himself in bad circumstances, repeatedly. When you were a soldier, they told you killing people was heroic. When you were an enforcer, the mob said you did your duty when you squeezed a lowlife for money owed. As a hit man, the people you were sent to kill were killers themselves. You don't kill civilians and kids are considered holy and off limits.

You've killed for money, in self-defense and as a preemptive strike. The pleasure you take in your work comes from winning and knowing you're taking out someone who deserves it. Now you only answer to Chill, yourself and God (in no particular order) and you're okay with it.

An ex-girlfriend once asked what made you okay with your job. You told her that no one you killed was destined to cure cancer. Regular people look down on guys like you, but you're making the world a more beautiful place. You are the garbage man.

Reles is about power and you're about justice. You'll cling to that distinction to your dying breath to stay righteous, just in case anybody really is up in the sky, counting your sins in a big ledger. You hope they count the sorrows you corrected, too.

"What else did Legs tell you?" Reles asks.

"She said she's going away for a long vacation. Greece, maybe."

He grimaces. "When?"

"I don't know. She has these big, burly men with her. Nice looking fellows. I'd love to be part of her entourage. Imagine getting to be with Legs Gabrielle all the time. A woman like her could turn a guy like me *straight*, honey!"

"Yeah."

He tips his hand. "How many big, burly guys was she with, Armando?"

You tell Reles you saw six men with her.

"Six?"

You went overboard trying to discourage him from bothering the client. "It was a tight squeeze back there, but that's how I got such a good whiff of that lovely perfume."

"Lavender, huh? I'll have to get some of that for my lady."

Reles gets up. "Bye, Mr. — "

"Armando, please!"

"Sure. *Armando*. Heh. When you prance back to Mr. Chillie Gillie, tell him Detective Hank Reles says hello."

RT ALL IT TAKES IS ONE MISSTEP AND YOU'RE SHIT ON TOAST. @ASSASSINSPLAYBK

"What gave me away?" you ask.

"Three things: First, when I was rude to you, you should have bitched me out more and left in a huff. Instead, you stayed. Why? Because you're here for something else. Me. Second, *six* guys? I've followed her around. I know how many guys are on her security detail."

A power sander won't do the job. You want to wipe the smug off his face with the rear tires of your car. You did that once to a guy in Chicago and it proved very satisfying. "What was the third thing?"

"You asked me what gave you away. That's when I knew for sure you've got to be a snitch for Gillie Security Associates."

"Shit." Your head heats up. You've used that same trick. Now you know how he got over on the qualifying interviews for the LAPD. Most monsters are stupid. He's not. He knows the right thing to say to get what he wants and no one understands how dangerous he is until he peels back the mask. Reles frightens you in a way few men do. He might be as good at his job as you are at yours. He might be better.

"Tell Legs I look forward to meeting her again. Tell her to drive carefully. I'm always watching...out for her." He stands over you, smiling. "Oh, and, Armando? Did you know that...I think, last time I checked, sixty-two people have died from pepper spray? Sixty-two! Probably more. I wonder how many pepper spray cans it would take to kill you? You'd be begging for death a long time before it would actually happen."

"Hypothetically?"

He shrugs. "Sure. Hypothetically, I could use MK-9. That might speed up the experiment. Heh. That's military grade pepper spray. I'd start with your eyes, of course. They say you throw up for hours with MK-9. After the first bit, there's nothing to throw up anymore and all you know is pain. It's like your eyes and nose and mouth and stomach are on fire but it doesn't stop. Hell must be filled with MK-9 and napalm. That's the fire that burns and burns but never consumes so the pain just goes on and on and it feels like an eternity until your heart gives out."

"Yeah, yeah. Mr. Policeman is our friend, but to me and Legs, you're just another pest going through the garbage who needs to be put down."

His laugh is that of a very convincing robot. "If I ever see you again, I am going to do things. You can't even imagine how bad."

"I've got a pretty good imagination."

"Good. Stay out of my way."

"You know that's not going to happen."

"Then I'll catch you later...*Armando*."

He's out of earshot by the time you think to reply, "I look forward to when next we meet, Professor Moriarty."

That would have been a pretty cool retort if it had come to you fast enough, but you were busy sweating. You make a mental note to pick up bottles of Pepto Bismol, just to have on hand in case you have to pour it into your eyes and mouth to neutralize a pepper spray attack. Milk or Coke will do in pinch, but the pink stuff is best. Now that you've met Reles face-to-face, you're sure you have to make more elaborate and desperate plans of attack.

It's not just that he's a very bad dude threatening a nice lady that spurs your fear for her. Despite all you've done, the fact that this asshole is supposed to serve and protect pisses you off. You used to serve. Sure, you're a hit man, but that doesn't make you a dick. Reles is a disgrace to every other decent guy in uniform.

Gay improv didn't work so when next you meet Hank Reles, you won't be Armando Delgado, non-threatening snitch. Next time you'll be badass.

RT SOME NIGHTMARES DON'T EVER GO AWAY. @ASSASSINSPLAYBK

Legs Gabrielle's house isn't the monster mansion you expected. A very successful cardiothoracic surgeon could live here, but it's far from Johnny Depp-level housing. It's not exactly small, but it's not hidden and anonymous behind tall, impenetrable hedges and razor wire, either. The house has four bedrooms and the piano-shaped pool out back stands drained and dry.

You look for Chill in the gathering crowd but he's not here yet. Glasses clink and drinks flow and someone fires up *Play that Funky Music (White Boy)* by Wild Cherry. Under different circumstances, you'd love to dance. Instead, you plug in your earpiece with the coiled wire and find out who else from Gillie Security Associates has arrived to deal with the influx of strangers parking in the circular driveway.

The driveway is full and people park up and down the road, wander in out of the dark and come through the open front gate. You had to park up the road too far and no one's checking IDs, so the situation is already out of

70

control.

"This is Fix on the perimeter," you say. "Check in."

"Two. Check. In the foyer." That's Berb.

"Three! Check. In the kitchen." That's Jeremy, the big Samoan bodyguard (and too loud in your ear.) He has the look needed for intimidation gigs. Babysitting celebrities is often about having the steroid freak or the fattest and tallest out front. A show of potential force eliminates the need for violence in most cases.

Jeremy is green. Last month, he was a repo man in Pasadena. He's shaped like a barrel and he either wants to stake out the kitchen or be where the ladies are. He's one of those guys who aspires to be a rapper and he seems to think he could do a better job guarding beautiful women by sitting beside them in hot tubs.

Chill caught him flirting with a client too hard last week. The Samoan was then tasked with walking yappy little dogs that fit in Louis Vuitton purses. Chill handed Jeremy a wad of plastic bags and told him to make sure he didn't forget to stoop and scoop. Jeremy snarled, "Yes, Mr. Miyagi. I'll paint your damn fence."

Everybody laughed, even Chill. Then Jeremy got more errands and yappy little dogs to stoop and scoop after.

You told Jeremy he didn't have to stoop and scoop.

"Really?" he asked, his pumpkin head split into a Jack-o'-lantern grin.

"The yard, yes. You have to clean that up, sure. But if the Reality TV star of the moment has a happy, snappy little Brussels Griffon that shits in her purse, that's not your responsibility. Don't go sniffing women's purses, kid."

Jeremy stared blankly. The kid doesn't get your sense of humor yet.

71

"Four," Skunk whispers, "In the front main room."

It seems like a long time has passed since you handed Sugar, wrapped in one of Oswald's blankets, over to the oldest of the crew. Skunk will be hanging back, trying to blend in with the curtains, watching eyes and hands and memorizing faces.

No word from One. That's Chill. In his absence, you give the orders you're sure he would issue.

"Three, head upstairs and keep people out of the bedrooms. We don't want any plants in there. As soon as the party's over, somebody has to stay up and go through the whole house to scan for bugs and cameras. You guys draw straws to see who stays up all night and tomorrow."

There's no hesitation. Berb congratulates Jeremy. "I've just drawn straws and it's low man on the totem pole again."

"Aw!" Jeremy's mouth seems to be full of potato chips.

"Clear the channel. One will be listening," you say. "All hail One."

"Hail," each guard says in sequence.

If Chill has arrived and is parking his car, he's not laughing.

You don't recognize any of the actors — this must be the wannabes and B actor brigade — but you recognize a comedian named Redban coming up the driveway. He's sharing a joint with a young woman who, by her look and dress, is a porn star before the anger and sadness has kicked in. Between her giggles, you catch the first half of a joke he tells onstage about dating Asian girls.

You envy his confidence. Tia Marta beat your confidence out of you and, given what happened with your last two girlfriends, you're in no hurry to hook up with the next one.

You circle the perimeter, but with no walls and no cameras, there's nothing to even slow any intruder who wants to slip in with the party goers. Legs seems destined to be a big star, but since she hasn't gone full legend yet, she's actually harder to protect. Most big stars have compounds and a full-time security staff that lives on the premises. The smart celebs who are running really hot don't go out in public much.

Chill sometimes gives fatherly lectures to some of his youngest clients. When they tire of being surrounded by security, they need to know that one day they'll be able to go to the grocery store without being mobbed. He tells them to send a maid for errands and enjoy the easy money while it lasts. When the fame goes away, and it almost always does, it's cold outside of the limelight.

Old bodyguards don't retire. They just hope to get shot. Chill gives work to some old buddies in the business sometimes. He assigns them to be paid friends to former celebrities who don't really need protection anymore. When celebs are young they don't really want to bother with security. After the trends cast them aside, those same celebs sometimes miss the image that having bodyguards projects.

Legs is on the upswing now and, seeing her onstage tonight, it's impossible to imagine she'll ever lack attention (the good type of attention that pays and the stalking kind that pains).

Chill's team is inside the house watching Legs so you play wallflower and hang around outside. Since the party has just started, everyone's inside raiding the bar. The pool is drained of water so the patio isn't very attractive and there are only a couple of people out here.

How will Reles come at Legs? You suspect you've made a tactical error. The easiest thing in the world is to walk up behind someone and pull a trigger. However, Reles doesn't want to kill Legs. He wants to possess her. He's the kind of cat who only kills the mouse after he's done tormenting it.

Chill has been holding you back since the events in Chicago, insisting you can find more peaceful ways to deal with assholes. Until today, you've managed pretty well, coloring within the lines. But remembering the look in Reles's eyes, you feel like an eager dog on a choke chain. When you see a guy like Reles wreaking havoc and terrifying a woman whose only crime is trying to entertain people, you want to use the Russian mines on him. Erasing the asshole would be easy, but dealing with more attention from the FBI would not. The Russian mines are leftover prizes from your Chicago adventures, stored away in a relatively safe place. One of those Russian beauties might be an easy way to blow up Reles in his car...or on his toilet. That would be good. Everybody poops.

You wonder about the girl in the chair. Is her body fully incinerated yet? Her horror gives you a familiar bout of nausea. That room reminded you too much of Miami. Rats crawled over your naked body in the dark, waking you with a start from fitful sleep and tortured dreams. The nightmares kept coming long after you got out of that basement.

You wish the recon in Montecito could have gone differently, but leaving a crime scene intact would be a gift to CSI nerds. There should be evidence of what those men did, but what could trip them up could also lead the police your way.

Justice for Reles and his friends is up to you. You had better go inside and talk to the client to find out what she knew that led you to the crime scene that will haunt your dreams.

RT JESUS AGREES. NO CAPES!
@ASSASSSINSPLAYBK
#THEINCREDIBLES

When you spot Legs by the bar, she has changed into a long white sheath slit up one side to display one of her famous gams. She's surrounded by a clutch of friends and admirers, but her eyes get big when she spots you. Chill must have described you to her. You give her a wink and a nod. With numerous apologies, she extracts herself from the center of the group quickly. In a moment, she joins you on the terrace overlooking the backyard.

"Great set tonight."

"Thanks!" Her eyes are bright. "Mostly, when guys say 'great set,' they're staring at my tits."

"I'll do that, too, but I'll be sneaky about it."

She nods. "Comedy is the best high there is and I've tried a bunch." She holds up her champagne flute in a little toast and smirks, "Better than this stuff. I got this bubbly for thirty bucks and it tastes like five. Somebody stomped the grapes with dirty feet. The toe jam makes it too sweet."

"Nice."

"So you've got to be Dr. Fix."

"Right now? I'm just the babysitter. J.D. to my friends. You can call me J.D."

"Chill calls you his Agent in Charge of Special Projects."

"Sounds better than Thug in Charge of Dirty Tricks, doesn't it? I've asked Chill if I could go by Emissary of Righteous Vengeance."

"He wouldn't go for it?"

"He wouldn't buy me a cape, either. Chill said capes are gaudy, though making him say 'emithary' ith fabulouth!"

"Don't be mean. I love his lisp...*hith lithp!* It softens him a little. Besides," she adds, "You're a couple of centuries too late to rock a cape. That look rarely works in modern life."

"So, I guess this is a bad time to ask if you're a Marvel or DC fan."

"Batman and Superman have it wrong — "

"Sacrilege!"

She shrugs. "Like in *The Incredibles*, you'd strangle yourself to death in a revolving door or something."

You take in her high cheekbones and full lips.

"You're staring," she says.

"Sorry. Women who are fans of *The Incredibles* are sexy. Just putting that out there." Jeremy the Samoan can't get away with flirting with clients, but you figure you're mildly cuter. You've always been shy around women, but gorgeous women do make you aspire to extroversion. Given that she already has a stalker who packs heat, you pause to consider that your timing is lousy.

Legs Gabrielle's smile is tolerant but she lets the

moment pass so you move on briskly. "Really funny stuff tonight. There aren't many comediennes, but you sure stand out." Your mistake.

"Cut that shit," she says. "Women in comedy don't like that. We're just comedians or comics. Comedienne sounds like something Elayne Boosler had to put up with when she was breaking ground. That ground's broke." Seeing you look stricken at offending her, she softens. "Besides, I prefer the term 'Professional Goofist'."

"And do you prefer actor or actress?"

"So far, I'm mostly a screamer in a tank top in B horror movies. Most critics would say the label of actor or actress applied to me is an insult to real thespians."

"You know what they say about thespians, Miss Gabrielle? A lot of girls just experiment with thespianism for a semester or two in college."

With that stupid joke you make a movie star laugh. Most comedians have to feel like they're the only ones in any room who can get a laugh, so you decide not to put it off: you like Legs a lot.

"I thought you'd be taller," she says.

Okay, you like her a little less. "I get that a lot."

"People dare to call you short a lot?"

"Oh…gee whiz. Up until now, I thought they were just quoting the line from *Roadhouse*. Everybody tells Patrick Swayze's character — "

"Dalton!"

"Yeah! Everybody tells him they thought he'd be taller."

She touches your arm and you feel better about the world. "*Roadhouse!* Man, I love that movie!"

Legs is a funny movie star who loves *Roadhouse*. You promised yourself you wouldn't fall in love so easily again, but your shields are down. "Everybody loves that movie," you say, "but no one is supposed to. It's not allowed. I love it non-ironically, though."

"I know what you mean. I hate it when people call my work 'a guilty pleasure.' They bought the ticket and they laughed their asses off or at least they had a good time. I can't stand critics who think they could do better or worry that they shouldn't have enjoyed themselves. The pricks."

She looks up and her cheeks redden. "Sorry, J.D. I know nobody gives a shit about lucky white girl problems. I had a weak moment of honesty there. When I win the Oscar someday, I'll try to remember people are starving in Africa."

"Heavy is the head that wears the diamond tiara," you say.

She smiles and you want to see more of that so you risk going back to the well and add, "Golly, though! I'm short? This is terrible news! I thought I was tall since my legs reach all the way to the ground."

She cracks up a little, but it could be the cheap champagne.

"My God! Apparently I'm a little person and I didn't notice until now!" To your immense relief, Legs cracks up again. Her easy laughter encourages you.

"But me and Patrick Swayze? We're *strong* dwarves." You strike a pose and flex a bicep.

It wasn't that funny, so she's probably nervous around you. You try to set her at ease with a nod to her world. "I might have an okay bit if poor Patrick Swayze wasn't dead. I guess I'll have to hold off a bit longer on my dreams of doing stand-up, at least until I update my material."

"A guy like you…sorry, you're not what I expected. You're so thin."

"I prefer 'wiry.' Most guys who work security details just slap a mean look on their faces, like they just ate barbecued baby and are hungry for a juicy toddler." You shrug. "Cliches are so…"

"Cliche?"

"Right."

She toasts you and takes a gulp of the bubbly. Her gaze moves to the gate, wary again and searching. Reles might be out in the dark, watching her from the deep shadows under the trees.

Legs has not asked about Oswald. Chill probably told her she doesn't need or want to know the details of what you do. She's an actress, so you can't be sure, but she must not know about the fire you set today. Not yet.

All you want to do is talk to her about comedy and superhero comics and *Roadhouse*. Instead, it's time to move past the introductory pleasantries. She sent you to a monster's house and four people are dead, three by your hand. What's her connection to the dead girl in the chair?

RT WHEN QUOTING #HIGHLANDER, I OFTEN SOUND MORE LIKE PETER LORRE. @ASSASSINSPLAYBK

"I went to Chill about Reles. I've had plenty of stalkers, but he's the only one who scared me. I wanted him out of my life, but I couldn't figure out how. He said he had a guy for that."

"That's me. Raccoons and roaches are my business."

"Huh?"

"Raccoons, I discourage from coming around and I keep them out of your attic. We started calling stalkers 'raccoons' because they're always going through celeb garbage looking for toenail clippings and whatnot."

Legs asks you for details about your job.

Working security assignments in Hollywood is much safer compared to the dangers of your last gig. That included running guns and trading in Russian mines with evil people, plus explosions and nearly burning to death.

Blending in with a crowd of anxious, autograph-seeking fans standing behind a velvet rope? Until today, most of your work in Hollywood has been easy. You skip the details that include blood and bone and give her a summary of the light lifting you do.

"I discourage stalkers, often using their own douchebag tactics. They go through celeb garbage so I go through theirs, for instance. I'm the garbageman. Somebody cyber stalks you, I cyber stalk them right back, but harder."

Using some of the less subtle intimidation techniques you learned back East? That's called 'going Jersey' and it's better than working a retail job and trying to sell khaki pants to hipsters for a few bucks an hour at The Gap.

You leave 'going Jersey' out of your story, too. "Chill sometimes slips me anti-stalker assignments. Occasionally, I do some undercover bodyguard work."

"What's an undercover bodyguard?"

"That usually involves hanging out in malls, protecting the teenage children of celebs. They aren't aware they've got a bodyguard unless there's trouble. Kids like the idea of bodyguards. They even brag about needing us. That's the first week. Then they want to go to the movies with their friends and not worry we'll tell their parents they're having sex or smoking pot. The parents still worry about kidnapping, so I sit in the dark and watch kids watch movies."

"And do you watch them have sex and smoke pot?"

"I'm discreet," you say. "Speaking of discreet, you shred anything that has phone numbers, bank records... anything personal that could be used against you, right?"

"Dude! I've met enough creeps and paparazzi, I run my tampons through the shredder before I throw them out."

"Tampons. Yeah. When fans turn to fanatics, things can get really weird."

As a former mob enforcer, you're still having a hard

time adjusting to your new lifestyle. You have a little money set aside now, thanks to Chill, but you can't go out and spend it on much that's fun. Movies are okay because you can slip into a darkened theater and maintain your low profile. Walking up and down Rodeo Drive in Armani and Ray-bans, you manage to fit in. However, you are still a fugitive and that means living off the grid.

You don't have to turn caveman to elude the Feds, but you have to be so ridiculously careful that sometimes you think life would be much easier if you went full Harrison Ford in *Witness* and hid out among the Amish. Building barns wouldn't be so bad if you could fall in love with a hot chick in a bonnet.

"You said roaches and raccoons. What do you mean when you say 'roaches'?"

That's your segue. "Reles is a roach. He needs to be stepped on. How'd you meet Hank Reles, Miss Gabrielle?"

"He came to one of my parties. He tagged along with Ross Oswald. He's my agent's accountant. Mort's my agent."

"Mort Sheldrake?"

"You know him?"

"I know the name."

She spoke of Oswald almost as an afterthought. She doesn't have to know the slime is now burning in the land of the past tense. That knowledge will have to wait. You'll let Chill break it to her that you had to go into extermination mode. When this is over, you'll have to disappear for a while. Maybe you'll drive up the coast to Seattle and let things cool down. You could drink coffee and…what else do people do in Seattle?

83

"You're very worried about Reles," you say. "What did he say to you?"

"He told me he likes the way I scream in the movies," Legs says. "He said he'd like to make me scream like that. I'm tortured and die in the movie he loves most."

"*The Tar Pit Killings?*"

"You've seen it?"

"Piece of shit," you say and the muscles around her mouth go slack. "Uh, sorry. Horror movies with torture aren't my sort of thing. I'm not saying everybody has to hate it, but I've got a sore spot." For instance, you've still got a sore spot over your right kidney where a bad guy thumped you with the butt of his sawn off shotgun.

What you don't say is that you've endured too much real torture to ever get some kind of vicarious thrill through a cheap horror movie. "But I heard you were great in it," you hasten to add.

Legs breaks into a laugh. For such a delicate looking woman, her laugh is full-throated and raucous. "You're from back East, aren't you?"

"Yeah."

"Where?"

You do your best Christopher Lambert impression from *Highlander* and say, "Lots of places." It comes out more like Peter Lorre and she's confused.

"I'm sorry, Miss Gabrielle. I forgot my manners. I was supposed to give you the Hollyweird answer and say you were, 'Simply fabulous!'"

You love her easy smile. If you hadn't sworn off falling in love recently, Legs Gabrielle could definitely be The Future Mrs. Diaz. If she could read your thoughts, she'd call you a crazy stalker, too. You'd have to shoot yourself

84

in the face.

"I so rarely hear honesty," Legs replies, "that whenever I hear it around here, it's like the person speaking has lapsed into another language."

"No offense taken?"

"No, no. Thanks for the slap of cold water. I'm from Maine. I'm used to cold water. *Tar Pit* did suck. I told them so at the time."

"Obsequious hipster suck ups are supposed to say you were fabulous. Failing that, how about I give you a line? I look forward to you starring in movies that are worthy of your talent."

"Hipster douchebags don't know what 'obsequious' means," she says, "but people toss so much bullshit my way, especially men, they must think I'm a mushroom and they're trying to make me grow."

That seems to remind her of something and her smile fades again. "I deal with flirts and fans all the time, J.D. I never have a problem because I usually stick them with a joke or, if they get too mouthy, I treat them like a heckler in the club. That won't work with this guy. Hank Reles is something else. Something…"

"Less than human."

"I was about to say that."

"It's all in the eyes," you say. You've seen Reles's marble gaze. You recognize the fear in Legs Gabrielle.

Her instincts are correct.

RT A LABRADOODLE IS BETTER THAN A LIFE OF PROSTITUTION. @ASSASSINSPLAYBK

A couple of peroxide blondes holding champagne flutes approach, their eyes on Legs. Their eyes have that star struck look that says, *I'd go lesbo for one night for bragging rights.* A couple of guys trail them, their gaze fixed on the girls' asses. They look like eager frat boys who've stumbled into the Playboy Mansion.

You do a half-turn and give the group your mean look and a dismissive wave of your hand. They get the message and veer off.

"Why did you ask Chill to get me to check Oswald's house if it's Reles you're worried about?"

"There was this girl. I was worried about her. Oswald didn't treat her well. Neither did Reles. I tried to be tolerant for a while because they were Mort's friends, but...people make choices. They've got their lives, but that doesn't mean I have to see it."

"Be specific."

"The girl was one of those high-priced escorts, the

classy kind you spot with old rich guys with faces like raisins. Watch any Academy Awards and you can play spot the john. Something Mort said about Oswald and this girl he brought to the parties…it set me off."

"What did Mort say?"

"I forget the exact wording, but it set off alarm bells. Something about treating a whore like a whore and that's what they're paid to do. Then Reles said her work was no different from any actress but the hours were shorter."

"Is Mort tight with Reles?"

"He said Reles was his bodyguard."

"Agents only need guarding from their clients."

"I think Mort likes a posse. It's about getting girls for each other."

"Nothing shadier than that? Anything worse than hiring hookers, for instance?"

She looks confused. She has no idea how ugly and deep this goes. She still thinks this is about Reles and his obsession with her. It's about Ginger and who knows how many more young women tied to chairs in the dark.

Someone's got to the stereo. The music is *Celebration* by Kool & the Gang. It doesn't fit the mood on the terrace.

"Mort called this morning to tell me he had a big gig for me, but if I wanted it, I'd have to go to a private party at Oswald's house. I declined. Then Oswald called me up. Mort must have given him the number or it's in my tax paperwork. Anyway, Oswald said, 'Be an actress for us.' I got his meaning."

"And you knew that meant sex."

She nods. "At least sex. I'd talked to the escort a lot. She was actually a nice girl. She came to L.A. looking for work in the movies like all of us do. I could have been her. Lots of girls could have been her. Everybody's gotta pay the rent. Last I saw the girl, she said she was thinking of getting out of the business. It was getting too rough, is what she said."

"What did you tell Mort?"

"We'd already fought about Mort's friends — Reles and Oswald. I didn't want them to come around to my parties anymore. I'm so pissed at Mort, I'm looking for new representation. That's why I got back onstage tonight. Mort didn't want me to play around onstage. Said stand-up was hurting my brand. He said directors were looking for a more demure me."

"What was the name of the girl who worked as an escort?"

"Called herself Ginger. Nice young woman. Sugar introduced me to her. Sugar hung out with Oswald, too. She was a working girl, but I thought she had designs on graduating to trophy wife. Don't get me wrong. She's nice, but she acted like she enjoyed Oswald's company more than Ginger did."

Maybe Legs is right about Sugar's demeanor. Or maybe call girls have more in common with actresses than Legs knows. The lovely, terrified Asian woman didn't look like she had any love for Oswald when you found her locked in his cage.

"Were there other girls?"

"There was a string of them with Oswald. Sugar must have been a favorite since she lasted the longest."

"What can you tell me about Ginger?"

"Not much. She liked dogs. She wanted to buy a labradoodle puppy. She told me she was thinking about moving back East somewhere. Home, I guess. Haven't seen her in weeks. I hope she did move back home. I don't think she was cut out for the life she was trapped in. I offered her money to go back home. She said she had money and she'd save up. Just a couple more months she said, and she'd leave."

The dead girl in the chair. Half her head was shaved. The other half was long red hair. And the somewhere she never made it back to was Indiana. The dead girl in the chair was Tabitha Bernstein, dog lover. She'd been a person with dreams and a life and a name before Oswald and Reles got to her and erased everything. There are several names on the list Oswald gave you, and that trash has to be taken out, Garbageman.

You close your eyes. You see the dead girl in the chair again. She raises her head and blinks at you. She says in a whisper, "Makes you want to paint the town red with blood, doesn't it, Jesus?"

RT HINCKLEY WAS FOCUSED ON @STEPHENKING FIRST. @ASSASSINSPLAYBK

Legs filed a complaint against Reles. The policeman she spoke to doubted her and didn't even want to file a report on the detective. "The detective told me that, even if what I say is true, the best course of action is to ignore Reles and hope he goes away."

"Chill finds that can be a point of contention with cops. It's true that many stalkers move on if ignored and you shouldn't engage them. Remember John Hinckley Jr.?"

"The nut who tried to impress Jodie by killing Reagan? Of course. I'm slightly older than I look but I'm also much smarter than I look. Besides, I know Jodie."

Sometimes you forget that many of Chill's clients don't think of movie stars as movie stars. They're the people they hang out with on golf courses or know personally from the set. They watch each other's kids from the sidelines at little league.

To you, every big star's name is a unit: first name, last name. Jodie Foster is Jodie Foster. Miss Foster, maybe, but just Jodie? Never.

"Uh, Jodie Foster, yes…" you say finally. "What a lot of people don't know is, Hinckley was focused on Stephen King and some other celebrities first. Stalker psychology is variable. It can take them a while to decide on their target. Sometimes attention from law enforcement, restraining orders or a simple reply to a fan letter actually encourages them. Still…"

"Still, what?"

You take a deep breath and lay it out for her. "The official line is not to pay too much attention to stalkers or they suck you into their psychodrama. They become sure they've got a relationship with you. They go to great lengths to rationalize their actions, even if it means breaking into your home. Some stalkers focus on their idols for years."

She studies the carpet, losing hope again. "The same psycho was focused on Dave for a long time and kept breaking in," she says.

"Dave?"

"Letterman," she answers. "I tried to be nice to Reles, but I was firm when I turned him down."

"It's not your fault, Miss Gabrielle. He's bent. You could have spit in his face and he would have taken that as a come on. It sounds like he did get your message. You aren't interested, so then he decided to come at you sideways. From the information I gathered today, it looks like these men have a…well, I don't know how else to say it. They treat all women like whores."

"And actresses…" she says. "I should have seen the signs earlier. Since that first party Reles acted like a creep. I would have kicked him out earlier, but he was part of

Mort's entourage. Everywhere I went after the first night I met him — over two months ago — it feels like someone's watching me. Just when I think I'm not being followed, I turn around and there he is again, watching and smiling. He's been following me around, off and on, for weeks. I wonder sometimes if he's just sitting out there in his car jerking off or if he's getting up the nerve to come and shoot me in the face or...or...make me scream for him like I did in that movie. I should have seen it coming earlier."

"The first thing to keep in mind at all times is that the stalker is the psycho, not you. You aren't crazy and you did nothing to invite this."

She looks unconvinced and distracted, her eyes searching the dark uselessly again.

"A few years ago, there was a story out of Jersey," you offer. "A supermarket chain cranked up a new policy to try to make their stores friendlier. They told the staff on the cash registers to smile more, call customers by the name on their frequent shopper card. It was supposed to be innocuous, public relations stuff to get people to shop at their stores more."

"Did the customers go into shock? You said this happened in Jersey? Polite cashiers must have freaked some of them out."

"Maybe, but the big issue that emerged were a lot more problems with male customers. Some of the old ladies didn't like it because getting called by name in a line up at the supermarket felt too personal, like the lower classes were taking liberties with them. But the men? A bunch of them looked at these young female cashiers suddenly smiling at them and they thought the checkout girls were trying to pick them up, even hideous old guys."

"It's not my fault. Thanks. I get it. But it is my problem. What else can you tell me about stalkers?"

You shrug. "It's often a no-win situation. If you aren't responsive, you're a bitch. Some think they're helping you. Or their career will be boosted up. Or they think you'll rescue them from their messed up lives. They want money and love. They're narcissists starved for attention."

"The detective I talked to...he said I could try to take out a restraining order but he said some things — "

"Restraining orders are made of paper, not Kevlar, so their resilience under the strain of bullets is a shade low. Also, most cops would acknowledge that stalkers have a worrying tendency toward threat escalation. Today's Peeping Tom is tomorrow's panty sniffer and, if they don't get derailed, eventually they can become rapists or worse. They start out small, building up their nerve. If the stalker breaks into your house, of course, the police can haul him away, but mostly, police are for after — "

You shut off that sentence before you get to the end of it and clear your throat. Honesty is fine, but she's already plenty scared. "Trouble is, there's a double standard. Even with high profile clients, the cops figure you've got your own security, a ton of fans or fanatics and most stalkers go away or lose interest if *you* go away. Careers are often short in Hollywierd and maybe the cops are trying to manage their caseload by attrition."

Her eyes are focused on you again. Despite the topic, it gives you a warm feeling. "What's the double standard?"

"If you were the President of the United States, the Secret Service doesn't wait around to see if the threat is viable. They go interview suspects and get in their face with a threat assessment and stern words." You smile. "Maybe more than stern words."

"Okay, but I don't want extra security around me all the time and forever. Your guys aren't bad. This isn't about them. It's just that extra security makes everything a hassle. If I want to go out, I have to plan ahead. I can't just jump in the car and go. I'm never alone and I feel like I'm under house arrest. This stalker is different. From this guy, I can never feel safe and just…I want to be left *alone*! The rest of my crazy life is already enough of a strain. This guy has already been in my house a few times with Mort and Oswald. It feels like a much more personal violation than a creepy fan letter from some guy writing all the way from Topeka."

A lot of people would exchange places with her without hesitation. Most wouldn't pause to say goodbye to their children if they could be her. You run your eyes over her body and reconsider. Most probably couldn't handle the ongoing borderline anorexia, heavy workouts and pressure it takes to be an up-and-coming starlet. It's not so rosy at the top and you know what it's like to have friends betray you. You want to give her a hug, tell her the truth and let her know that one of the monsters is already dead and gone. The rest are on your list and you're good at this sort of thing.

Of course, you can't do any of those things. Down here at the bottom sucks, too.

"The cop I talked to? It was more than just a case of one cop protecting another. He suggested that a restraining order might not fly. He said a judge probably wouldn't believe a rich bitch slut like me."

Your jaw goes slack. "You didn't go to the station, right?

You called the police and I'm guessing a guy named Mueller showed up at your door, probably without a partner, am I right?"

"Yeah. How'd you know?"

"Because the cop at your door wasn't representing the best and brightest and finest of the LAPD. He was repping for Reles."

"Shit."

"That's the name of the cop you spoke to, right?"

"Detective Mueller, yeah."

You don't have to add another target to your list of names. His name is already there. He doesn't know it yet, but he's a bowling pin. You're the ball.

Her eyes are wet. "I'm totally screwed, aren't I?"

"Not yet."

"This is a nightmare."

"Ever hear of a guy named Bekhti? Odd name. Stands out."

"No."

"We'll save him for last since we know the others. He'll turn up. Break a hornet's nest, they all come out to swarm."

"What are you going to do? There's a bunch of them."

"A handful. Slightly fewer than a bunch."

"We've got to call the FBI, right? This is going to tear up my life. I'll never be safe. What if Reles and Mueller have more friends?"

"That's the hell of it, Legs. Most cops take serve and protect very seriously. Some cops think that motto is all about them and their own. If you bring in the FBI, there's no way to tell which way the investigation will break. They might even try to bring you down, smearing you to silence you."

"What do I do?"

"Leave it to me."

"What can you do?"

She looks so scared, you want her to feel a little safer. You break a rule from your playbook and hope Legs can handle it. "I said I had names. There are fewer names now. Used to be a bunch."

RT THIS IS NOT A MOVIE. BAD THINGS HAPPEN TO HEROES. @ASSASSINSPLAYBK

You give Legs Gabrielle your best encouraging look. She's strong, but she's been pretending to be strong for a long time, like a rope pulled at either end by powerful, relentless machinery until it snaps. When Chill put you on the case, she thought J.D. Fix meant an easy fix. Finding out there's more than one cop involved? Twice as bad.

"Can you really stop these guys?" Miss Gabrielle asks.

"If I fail, I'll fail in such a way that they still won't bother you or anyone else again."

"What does that mean?"

"If things go bad…it beats dying old of tumors spreading out from the prostate." When they write your obituary, the headline will read: *He never worried about dying old.*

"Careful," she says. "Reles is a lot bigger than you. Mueller, too."

"No worries. I'll be a smart ninja. Every guy has to have a thing. That's my thing."

97

Brave, goofy words. Even as you utter them, your throat goes dry. You swallow with a hollow click. Words are as useless as an empty gun. What you haven't learned yet is that you aren't as brave as you think you are — certainly not as brave as you sound. The whole prostate cancer dare was bravado to impress a beautiful woman. However, you are just stupid enough to still believe macho bullshit. Deep down, you think the law of cause and effect won't apply to you. Laws are for suckers. You're the hero of your own movie so naturally you believe nothing really bad can happen to you. You share the same delusion as everyone else and so, when the surprises come, your suffering shall be all the more egregious.

When you begin to turn away, she catches you by the shoulder. "Chill said I shouldn't ask, but, did you find something we can use against Reles and his buddies? Is Mort involved?"

"I've got nothing on your agent besides the fact he sounds like a sewer rat. For the rest, when Chill says you shouldn't ask, don't. I've already told you too much. In fact, I was never here."

"But at least tell me you found Sugar. Is she safe?"

You allow a slight nod.

She sighs heavily. "Thank you. Did Ginger go back home?"

"Could be. Um…so, look, this thing has barely begun. We'll keep you safe, but all these people wandering in doesn't make it easy. We usually have to prepare for events like this."

"Sorry, but I feel safe in a crowd and another moment given up to fear makes me feel like Reles has already won. I can't stand anyone winning but me."

"What did Chill tell you, Miss Gabrielle? About me, I mean?"

"You say 'what'. You really mean 'how much.' From what Chill says, keeping me safe isn't your department. That's up to those other three. Mr. Berbniak didn't want me to have the party tonight, either —"

"How many people are coming tonight?"

"I think at some point I told you to call me Legs or... wait. You're about to tell me something unpleasant, aren't you?"

"Would you cancel tonight's party?"

"It's not a party, J.D. It's a get-together."

"Do get-togethers have guest lists?"

"No, that's a party thing. Parties have themes and caterers. At get-togethers, it's much less formal so somebody gets naked and drunk and ends up on TMZ."

"How do people know to come?"

"In my world, I tell one person and the cell phone tree takes over. We had a similar thing back in Maine when some idiot gets lost in the woods. The whole town comes out for a search and rescue. I prefer get-togethers, actually. With formal invitations, someone always gets left out and they get pissy and you have to take them to lunch so they still feel the love."

She drains the champagne from her glass and, as she tips her head back, you take that moment to admire her cleavage.

"In Maine, people are nosy and you hate them for it. Out here? People tell you everything. Why people need psychoanalysts anywhere on the West Coast is a mystery. They sure aren't holding anything back."

How you envy these people. You've got an ugly history

to "get over," whatever that means. You'll never live long enough to forgive the past.

RT THE DESERT IS HARD IN NEVADA. PICKS, NOT JUST SHOVELS. @ASSASSINSPLAYBK

"Can I tell you something else before I go?"

"Not if it's going to ruin my evening," she says. "I've had enough of that."

"Sorry. It's just that staying low profile is safer. Are you sure you can't get out of town?"

"And there goes the evening. I have security here: you're here and all my friends are here."

"Are they all your friends?"

Legs looks around and shakes her head. "There are people here I don't know. That's how get-togethers work. But aren't I safer surrounded by a crowd in my own house?"

"You'd think so, but no."

"This is ridiculous. I'm sorry, but I've given up enough time and headspace to Reles and his friends."

You catch her arm and give her your best smile. "Legs, I need to let you in on something. I really am trying to help you here."

She gestures with her empty glass to give you the floor.

"If I were a psycho cop who wanted to kidnap a star such as yourself — "

"Starlet, I think."

You give her a heavy sigh and she pays attention. "A couple of hours from now, when the party — the get-together, is really rocking, I'd phone in an anonymous noise complaint. I'd arrive, maybe with another cop who's a tight friend and maybe not. Maybe I'd have another accomplice in the crowd. That wouldn't be hard. Anyway, if I were him and I wanted to take you off in my cruiser, the accomplice would drop a baggie of cocaine on the coffee table in plain sight as I arrived to deal with the noise complaint."

"Is this how your mind works all the time, or are we just talking about Reles?"

"I'm picturing a scenario where you could easily end up locked in the back of a cruiser."

"I have lawyers."

"You're still thinking like a human, Legs. He could take you back to his precinct and have you all to himself for a while, far too long before your lawyers could spring you. But if I were him, I'd pull the same trick the NYPD pulled with Occupy Wall Street protesters. I'd take you to some far flung precinct so it would take longer to find you. All the while you're in processing, you're in handcuffs and maybe you're in a private interrogation room with the cameras turned off."

"Oh, God."

"They can do anything and get away with it. Whatever happens to you, they'd call it the consequences of resisting arrest. Or maybe Reles is really unhinged and he might

102

not take you to a police station at all. He might take you
for a ride all the way to Nevada and lose you in the desert.
Or he might take you down the coast and dump you off a
cliff into the Pacific once he's done with you. Guys like
Reles are unstable, so it's difficult for me to predict how
he'll react. The next move is his."

"You're scaring me."

"Only to protect you. I was thinking of holding back,
but now I think you should know the real deal."

"How do you get to be the guy who thinks like this?"

"Would you believe I'm a genius security strategist?"

"Maybe, but it would be simpler to assume you're
another psycho who just happens to be on my side.
Psychos are everywhere. Last month I auditioned for a
part and the director couldn't stop staring at my feet.
Breasts, I get all the time, but this dude was obsessed."

"Was it Tarantino? I understand he's into feet. I bet a
film student somewhere must be writing his graduate
thesis on the number of shots there are of Uma
Thurman's feet in *Kill Bill*."

"No, it wasn't Quentin and that was mildly amusing,
but," — a hard tone enters her voice — "I haven't
forgotten that when you talk about Reles, you sound like
you share his brain."

You try to look innocent, but does innocence look like a
shy smile or should you appear hurt by her accusation?
"According to Occam's Razor, the simplest solution is
probably the right answer, but quoting Occam's Razor is
something a brilliant strategist would say, so I can't help
you there. How I can help you is, please, call off the party
and let's batten down the hatches until I'm sure I've
discouraged Detective Reles. I haven't stuck a sword in the

bull yet. I've just waved a red cape at him."

"Just do your job, J.D. If the cops show up, we'll deal with them and I've got my lawyers on speed dial."

You reply, "Your lawyers are irrelevant to a guy like Reles unless they're well-armed." But you say it to her back.

She's already returning to her friends, back to that make-believe dimension where everything works out just fine, according to the script. However, before she's back inside she turns her head and freezes. She almost walks into the door.

You slide up beside her and follow her gaze. A man and a woman stand by the empty pool.

"Mort is here. I fired that son of a bitch this morning and he dares to show up at my own house with one of his girls!"

"Does Mort carry a weapon?"

"No. He's a shark. Isn't that enough? Watch out for his teeth."

"Keep calm. Stay inside. I'll speak with him."

"He's trespassing and he's an agent, not a cop. I can call the cops to get rid of him."

"No. Reles and Mueller might be waiting for that call so they can roll up and take you away."

"What will you say to him?"

"When I said I'd 'speak' with him, I didn't really mean I'd speak with him."

"This is my house. Don't hurt him. Not here."

"I promise. I won't hurt him."

You'll never be back here, so you take a chance. You put your arms around Legs Gabrielle and kiss her softly on the mouth. Surprised, she stiffens and then surrenders to you,

104

kissing back. It's an act to savor. A decade of her full lips on yours would be a good beginning.

Before you step off the terrace, you whisper in her ear, "You will never see me again, so remember this: you didn't set any of this in motion. You asked for help because *they* started this. I have the names. If you are ever tempted to feel sorry for any of these men, know that if you hadn't brought us in, you'd be their next victim. Whatever happens to them, it's for you and all the victims they've already made and all the victims they were going to make. Whatever happens is righteous and it's on me."

Her breath smells of champagne but her lips taste of strawberries. She puts her hands on your chest and gently, slowly pushes herself away.

Before you turn to deal with Mort Sheldrake you add, "And don't forget that kiss. I won't."

RT IN THE MOVIE, @JOHNLEGUIZAMO DOES IT. @ASSASSINSPLAYBK

Girls begin to dance with each other on the terrace, casting long, reaching shadows that play over Mort Sheldrake's face. He's kind of handsome. He might still be handsome, past the plugs that look like doll hair and the waxy look people get after too many facelifts. Not even Hollywood money can hold back time. He's a fit 55, looking like 45, but reaching for 35 using the questionable miracles of cosmetic surgery.

Sheldrake talks in low tones to a woman in a red dress. He speaks with an intense, staccato rhythm so you can hear the k's and t's.

You wander closer but at a tangent, just another party guest inspecting the empty pool. The pool is shaped like a piano. Berb told you some one-hit wonder owned this place before Legs and thought he was on the way up until the music industry collapsed and he had to sell the place to pay the IRS.

Sheldrake rings alarm bells but it's the woman who pulls your gaze. Her backless dress displays smooth skin, naked but for a tattoo of a jaguar prowling down the right side of her spine. She shifts from side to side but not in time to the music. She's either nervous or impatient. Her long black hair reaches down her back so the jaguar appears and disappears, appears and disappears.

The woman in the red dress shakes her head. "Don't!"

Sheldrake's face twists into an ugly snarl. He balls his fist and swings at her face. Just before his punch makes contact, he stops and steps close to give her a hug. She flinches in a way you recognize. That's someone who is used to being hit. You used to be like that. Learned helplessness is tough to break.

Then he does it again. His fist comes closer this time. When he steps into another hug, she turns so you catch half of her face in the light. That half is terrified and desperate so you take a wild guess and extrapolate the rest.

You clear your throat.

The guy looks over at you and smiles. "Don't need a drink right now, Jose."

"Ginger sent me."

That startles him. He pushes the girl back, focuses on you.

"Ginger? Ginger who?"

"That was weak. Try again."

"Who are you?"

"I'm Dr. Fix. I fix things. Ginger says you need to get fixed. I'm a vet. I can do that."

"When did she tell you this?"

"I met her late this afternoon."

"I don't think that's the same Ginger I know."

"Did you shave half her head? Or did you just help hold her down while Mueller or Reles — "

He shakes. Not just his head. His hands shake. His body trembles. It's fear, not rage, you see in his eyes. He's not an alpha dog in the rape and murder ring. He doesn't have the stones to be a leader. An innocent man wouldn't wear the face Sheldrake wears now.

"Did Reles tell you to do those things? Is that what helps you sleep at night? You were only following orders?"

"I don't know what you're —"

"You're a murderer, Sheldrake. A john, a pimp, and even, I'm told, a big time agent. What makes a thing like you? Are you a new thing? There are more serial killers than there used to be. Is it the Internet? Is that how sickos find each other?"

Sheldrake turns to the girl with the Jaguar tattoo. She's already slipped away. She runs down the driveway holding her six-inch stilettos high. Makes you smile. Another life saved.

"These things you think you know…"

"Oswald's dead. He died horribly."

"How do you know? When?"

"Earlier this evening. I know because I killed him."

His face does some interesting, subtle things, like it's fighting the paralyzing effects of all that Botox. Mostly his lips push in and out, trying to think fast in panic mode. No one thinks fast, or well, in panic mode.

"Is it money you want?"

"Rich people always think that."

"So…we can negotiate."

"You would think that, wouldn't you? However, you aren't Miss Gabrielle's agent anymore. I'm her agent."

"What?"

"I'm her Agent of Delicious Violence, Divine

Vengeance Division."

The guy moves in to push you back. The main mistake rich, white Hollywood douchebags make in these situations is that they don't really want to fight. Whatever confrontations they've been in always crank up slow. It starts with dirty looks and idle threats and slowly escalates to shouting about lawsuits. Even if the guy amps himself up enough to actually fight, he has to warm up to it and get talky. A gawking crowd must gather and his pride must be hurt before he risks his perfect teeth and bloodies his knuckles.

With sex, you start slow, slowly get faster and make it last as long as possible. Strategy in a fight is the opposite of sex: start strong, finish fast. No foreplay. Even in a boxing match, you start out with a couple of jabs and feel out the opponent. That's not the way to go here.

"Don't you know who I — ?"

You knock him sideways with your strongest punch, a right hook to his perfect jaw throwing your hip forward so all the weight of the punch is where it needs to be. His mandible goes sideways. He hasn't even put up his hands yet. With your left hand, you grab the knot of his tie and twist, turning off his air. You use the tie to pull him into the next two punches. His perfect Roman nose pushes off to one side. He still hasn't put up his hands but you give him one more hook to be sure those hands stay down.

Your father, Marco Diaz taught you about the button. A couple of inches in front of the ear is the temporomandibular joint. To allow for chewing, the jaw has to move. The same joint, the button, that allows humans to eat? That's a design flaw in combat. Marco called a vicious hook to that spot, "ringing the bell."

Buttons or bells, you swing on Sheldrake and put your hip behind it again. If he didn't know it before, he gets it now. All his life, Morton Sheldrake has been a fake tough guy.

You were going to finish him with an uppercut. Civilians might think that's overkill, but every fight must be won decisively. If a guy's jaw clicks every time he tries to chew steak, he'll cross continents to avoid meeting you again. However, you don't finish him with an uppercut because Legs holds your arm. She doesn't try to restrain you. Her touch is gentle. She's asking with soft fingers on your shoulder, *don't kill him.*

You open your fist and, placing your hand in the center of his chest, gently push him backward into the pool. He twirls in midair. He's so far gone, he does a Superman and doesn't have it in him to protect himself as his face meets the concrete. It's the deep end, about ten feet down.

"Without water, should we still call it a pool?" you ask. "It should really be called a hole until there's water in it."

"Oh, my God!" she says. "You said you wouldn't...you *killed* him!"

"Maybe he's not dead, but I hope he is because, if not, I'll have to climb down there, drag him up and toss him in again head first."

She winds up and slaps you as hard as she can, which is pretty hard. Sheldrake lets out a ghostly moan of agony.

"It's okay. See? He's okay. Hey! Sheldrake! If you live, tell 'em John Leguizamo did this to you!"

"Chill said you could deal with problems quietly! Chill said you're supposed to be some kind of ninja!"

You look up and the girls on the terrace have stopped dancing. They're staring at you, memorizing your description for when the cops show up, no doubt.

Legs heads for the house. You're about to leave when you see Detective Hank Reles step out of the dark. He's already spotted you and he's marching for you, his gun already out and pointed your way.

His first shots go wide, but not by much. You feel the breath of the slug as it passes your left ear, whispering death. You have practiced many clever replies and movie catchphrases in the mirror. All words abandon you now.

RT MICRO UZI. 28 ROUNDS PER SECOND. YES. THAT WOULD DO. @ASSASSINSPLAYBK

There's screaming and chaos in the house. Berb will be on top of Legs Gabrielle. Lucky guy. Skunk will be on his way and maybe Jeremy the Samoan will extricate himself from the refrigerator long enough to come to your rescue, but that's iffy. You might have to save yourself.

Before Reles can shoot again at close range, you throw yourself to the only cover there is: the pool. Mort is struggling to his knees when you land on his back. Some bones crack and give, but it's him, not you. He has cushioned your fall. Sheldrake doesn't even yell. The air goes out of him. He collapses into the concrete, silent. You roll to your back and pull him on top of you.

Reles appears at the edge, peering down at you, pointing his revolver. Mort makes for a pretty flimsy human shield. You key your mic.

"I told you if I ever saw you again, Armando, I'd fuck you up!"

"You don't want to do that!"

He shoots out a chunk of concrete by your head. "Yeah, I really do."

"*Witnesses*, genius! The cavalry is on the way! Security to the pool! Scramble!" You keep the mic open, but you're talking to Reles now. "Detective Hank Reles has just beaten the green shit out of a guest and he's got a gun!"

You dare to show him the mic at your wrist and the coil of wire to your earphone so he knows you aren't bluffing. "It's attempted murder right now. It'll be murder in a second."

You read somewhere that what makes a person smart is that they go through much the same thinking process as the average dummy, but faster. Reles works through the equation fast. He takes one last hurried shot at you and runs.

The bullet misses you, but takes Mort through that precious face he's been getting a Beverley Hills surgeon to tighten up all these years.

You roll Mort off and sprint to the shallow end of the piano, up the steps, and pull your SIG.

Berb shows up at your side, pistol drawn. Skunk appears on the terrace. He's pulled out his Micro Uzi, but looks disappointed he has no target to perforate at twenty-eight rounds per second.

"Client secure?"

"With Jeremy," Skunk barks. "Where'd he go?"

"I'd guess the road and to his car but back up Jeremy in case he doubles back."

As if in answer, a woman's high, anguished scream goes up from the house. That's soon joined by another woman's voice cutting through the night. The natural thing to do would be to run to the screams, but that's no way to proactively deploy forces. Skunk runs to check the commotion. You run for the gate. Keying your mic as you go, you order Berb to keep everyone inside and down. "If I see Reles, he'll be returning fire in this direction."

When you get to the road, it's lined with cars. The only sound is noise from the house you can't make out. It's all just inarticulate shouting. The quiet road is lined by trees. Cold steals over you and, standing out on the dark highway alone, you feel stupid and exposed. You're trying to keep your head, but you just ran out into the road without pause. You slip behind a black Yukon and crane your neck, afraid Reles is behind you and lining up his shot.

"Berb! Report! Did I bet wrong?"

"Reles is not here, Fix."

Speaking must have helped Reles zero in. You hear a guttural report followed by *spang!* Reles puts a hole in the truck's side.

You're relatively safe behind the engine block, but all he has to do is move to get a better angle. A hundred people with cell phones must be, at this moment, calling the cops. You're a fugitive in a gun fight with a cop. That scenario can't end well.

You move around the back of the Yukon until the macadam is under you and you can peer up the road. There's nothing to see but the outlines of cars so you fire a shot to let him know where you are and twist away. Two more shots smack the pavement behind you. You're moving up the side of the road, staying low and sprinting from car to car, hoping he'll get stupid and show himself.

That realization stops you cold. You're hoping a smart guy, trained with weapons, will do something stupid in order for you to succeed. You wait, try to get your breathing under control, and listen. You need back-up to outflank Reles. Chill should have been here by now. With any luck, he's almost here, ready to put holes in Reles's back with his big Redhawk.

Eyes darting, you pull out your phone and call Chill for help.

Chill's ringtone reaches your ears: *It's Raining Men* by the Weather Girls. You make out the outline of Chill's midnight blue Escalade two cars up. Chill didn't report in when he arrived. You already know you're going to get bad news when you open the door to Chill's ride. The question is, how bad will the news be?

RT FLOATING BOX OF SURVEILLANCE VEHICLES, NOT DUKES OF HAZZARD. @ASSASSINSPLAYBK

A black pickup pulls out fast, fishtailing. You run to Chill's Escalade and haul the door open. The dome light pops on and, out of habit, you glance in the back seat before you jump behind the wheel. Chill's beside you, his bald head bloody and his eyelids swollen closed. He's not up to a conversation.

You check the pulse at his neck. His chest rises and falls regularly. His pulse is strong but he's been beaten badly and blood's everywhere.

"Chill? I need you to wake up, man!" With two knuckles, you dig into his sternum, rubbing up and down hard. Chill stirs from the pain, but he doesn't come around, either.

You bark quick orders into your mic. "Berb, secure the client. Skunk, 10-2 out by the gate."

"10-4," Skunk replies.

"What's going on?" Jeremy asks.

Before you can reply, Skunk chews out the junior

116

bodyguard for you. "Watch the crowd from the stairs and don't let anyone up. Keep the channel clear unless you spot something suspicious."

You fish Chill's keys out of his jacket and leave the door open so he'll be easier for Skunk to find in the dark. You run for the gate.

Skunk is in your ear. "Who needs EMS?"

"Number One. He's in the back of his ride, just west of the gate. Door's open, no bad guys in sight."

"Roger that."

Skunk's still in your ear and you almost run into each other by the gate. You order Skunk to give you his keys. He doesn't hesitate and he points at his red Crown Vic a few cars down the road, parked so it's pointed back to the city. Good man.

Berb chimes in, but only to report, "Client's secure." His tone is flat and angry. There's something else in his voice, but you can only process so much at one time.

At Skunk's Crown Vic, you pause and use the pen light from your shirt pocket to check it before you jump in. No one's in the back seat waiting to brain you with a lead pipe. There's no time for this. The bad guy is getting away. You hop behind the wheel and gun the engine.

"Fix?" Skunk's breathing hard.

"How bad is he?"

"He's out. He's lost a lot of blood."

The road winds through the Hills. If you had time to check out your phone's GPS you'd have a better sense of where you are. You've rarely ventured into this part of Los Angeles and nothing looks familiar. Big, well-lit homes far from the road flash by here and there. To your right are sheer drops. To your left are tight corners you take at ill-advised speeds. There's a wonderful view of city lights from up here, but a moment's distraction will kill you. You were too far away to catch the license plate on the pickup so you have to catch up to Reles.

Horns blare as you pass slower vehicles and a couple of times you're forced to cut in quick to avoid a head-on collision. You hate this. Some guys love to race cars and learn to do donuts in high school parking lots. You never went to high school and the first thing you drove was an Army Jeep. The only vehicle you ever really enjoyed was a Humvee in the desert, government issue and armored up. There was a lot more room for error then, even when jumping a sand dune.

If you overtake Reles up in the Hills, you have a chance at getting him. Once he hits the rabbit's warren of city streets, he'll lose you easily. You press the accelerator harder.

This is no way to chase anyone. To do this properly, you should have five cars keeping him in a floating box of surveillance vehicles. Chasing people in a car is stupid. Better to pick them up when they aren't looking for you in the rearview mirror. With a car set up so the brake lights don't light up, you can even follow any bad guy surreptitiously from in front. Since he already knows you're after him and you don't have access to a helicopter, you're going at this all wrong, as if this is some kind of car chase from bad TV.

An ambulance roars past, lights and sirens all the way, climbing to rescue Chill. You click your body rig radio to let them know the paramedics are just minutes away, but all you get is static. You're beyond the broadcast range of Chill's crew. If you catch up to Reles, you forgot to pack another handy human shield. Your cell rings and you almost wreck as you dig it out of your suit jacket.

"Fix?"

"Kinda busy right now, Berb." You don't bother to explain. The squeal of your tires in that last turn should do that. "The client's secure, right?" Your pulse was already racing. Now it's a very fast drumbeat.

"She's not feeling very secure. In her bedroom, there's blood all over the walls."

"Shit."

"Some of that, too," Berb says. "How'd he get past us?"

"He must have already been in the house before the party started. I guarantee he was in the closet in the master bedroom, probably taking pictures of Legs as she changed into that fabulous dress." You catch an anguished cry in the background.

"Uh, got you on speakerphone, dude. Miss Gabrielle is right here."

The Crown Vic slides sideways too much on the shoulder and you almost tip. You wrestle the wheel, ease up on the gas and get the car back under control.

"Take me off goddamn speakerphone, Berb!"

"Done."

"Convey my apologies and assure Miss Gabrielle that when I catch Reles, I'll bring back his phone. I'll also present her with any pictures that are on said phone and whichever hand he jerks off with. Relay that just as I said it. She'll feel better."

"What's your location? Can you see the guy's vehicle? I'll call it in to the cops."

"Negative, boy scout. Call the cops to the house. I've got the takedown."

119

"Gotta be honest, it's pretty freaky here."

"Whose blood is on the walls? Have you found a body yet?"

"It's bad, but it's roadkill. He left a message in blood."

You hit a straight shot at the bottom of a hill and catch a glimpse of the black pickup ahead, turning left through a red light at the next intersection. You're out of the Hills and exactly where you don't want to be, careening though the city. "Don't keep me guessing. I hate a mystery. What's the message?"

"It says, 'Catch you later.'"

Those were Reles last words to you back at the cafe. He's playing, as if Legs's life is just a game and no one else matters. Is that a message to Legs alone, or is he putting you on notice, too?

"How do you know the blood's from roadkill?"

"It's still here. There's a dead raccoon in her bed."

"Uncool, dude. That'll spoil the mood."

RT #STARCHASE. IT'S A REAL THING. DRIVERS, SLOW DOWN. @ASSASSINSPLAYBK

You're almost on top of Reles when the lights and sirens fire up behind you. You turn on Skunk's police scanner and, naturally, they're talking about you.

"You got him?"

"Got him," the CHP cop behind you answers. "Now that I'm on him, pull over and see if he stops."

Under different circumstances, you would stop and hash this out. Those "different circumstances" include not being wanted by the FBI. If an officer of the law is going to decide about a difference of opinion between Detective Reles and a brownish Hispanic man such as yourself? You're going to get beaten senseless before you're murdered.

In the best case scenario, this chase ends with you shot or beaten. If you don't end up dead, they'll put you in a federal prison or in Gitmo wishing you were dead. The things you did right won't matter. They don't even have to charge you to keep you in a cage forever anymore if it doesn't suit them. Better write a new best case scenario fast.

Reles slows and pulls over like a law-abiding citizen. You give him the finger as you shoot past him. More sirens fire up and the police scanner chatters at you as more of the LAPD joins the chase.

You weave in and out of slower traffic — all traffic is slower than you tonight — but you've got no plan that could possibly end well. Not yet. Just as you're thinking you've got to lose them before they bring a helicopter into the pursuit, you hear the whir of rotor blades overhead.

The cop behind you speeds up close and tells you through his speaker to pull over. As if you didn't understand the premise of Cops and Robbers.

This couldn't get worse. At least you thought so until you hear a light thunk behind you. The cop on the scanner can't contain his enthusiasm when he says, "Got him! Starchase deployed."

Things just got worse.

A supervisor somewhere back there tells the officer in closest pursuit to back off. They've tagged the Crown Vic with a GPS stuck to the back with an epoxy compound. It sounds like something out of a sci-fi movie, but the LAPD have been using these little tattle tale devices since 2006.

You wrench the wheel right and head west. As long as you keep your speed high, they won't try to box you in. You weave right and left every few intersections so they won't anticipate where you're headed and set up a spike belt. They think they already have you, which is the only hope you have.

When you're speeding through city streets, it's difficult to wipe away your fingerprints. By the time you get to

Santa Monica Pier, the cops have lost patience and the helicopter's bright white searchlight beams down on you like the eye of God. The cruisers in pursuit hang back so maybe they're hoping you'll come to your senses and slow down, or at least run out of gas. If there were a busy mall, you could try to lose yourself there, but nothing nearby is that busy this time of night.

The police have got the copter and the tracker on you so they're trying to avoid pushing you to speed faster in the city. Prudent. You're driving crazy so you're very close to killing someone besides yourself. If you slow down, they might try a pit maneuver and bump you, forcing you to fishtail and spin out. If this chase goes on much longer, they'll try ramming you repeatedly.

You pull out your phone and dial Sgt. Billy. He doesn't answer. You call back, cursing him. You end up driving in circles and then figure eights, keeping your pattern unpredictable. Your pursuers will be smiling. In every other car chase they've ever been in, the perp was trying to get home. When they're in trouble, everyone heads home. You aren't an ordinary perp. You're a force for divine justice whose sidekick won't answer the fucking phone.

"Yeah?"

"Billy!"

"Yeah?"

"Why didn't you answer the phone?"

"I got a life. Havin' a bath."

"Me, too, in a minute. Get yourself to that place you like, not far from Santa Monica pier. As soon as you can."

"Why?"

"They've got good food."

"Anything else?"

"Bring donuts! Copy?"

"Yeah, yeah. Fine."

"I love you, Sergeant!"

"Oh, shit! It's serious!"

You hang up on him, grip the wheel and press the accelerator so Skunk's old Crown Vic roars as the new Interceptor engine broils under the hood. The floorboards are cut so the accelerator pedal can go a little deeper and open the monster's throat a little wider, delivering a little more punch. Skunk is going to be pissed about what you're going to do to his refurbished car.

RT HIT MEN PREFER NOT TO BE TAKEN ALIVE. BE A DENTIST, KIDS! @ASSASSINPLAYBK

It's so late, it's almost early, which is good because only a few young couples and late-night tourists wander the pier this time of night.

You lay on the horn and keep it pressed. You floor it again, heading straight out for the water. The Bubba Gump Shrimp company flashes by on your left. You've never eaten there and now you probably never will. There's a Ferris wheel back there. The last time you were on a Ferris wheel was Coney Island with your first real love and your best friend. If there was one good, uncomplicated day, it would be that one. You'll try to think of that in your last moments as you drown.

You arrested a Navy Seal for making trouble in a bar in Germany once. He told you that when he was trained, the other candidates drowned him. Every Seal got drowned and then resuscitated by the other trainees. As you put him in the drunk tank, he told you, "You get high from the lack of oxygen to your brain and feel euphoria when you stop struggling against the water." You hope he was telling the truth and that's not just macho bullshit.

You will not allow yourself to be taken alive. Whatever happens, you aren't going to prison and there's no macho bullshit about that vow. You spent years as a prisoner to two sadists as a kid. Prison or that terrible basement in Miami: it's all the same to you and you won't go through that horror again.

Maybe this end is as it should be. You should be dead several times over: Miami, New Jersey, New York, Chicago. You could have died many times. You should have treated this trip to California as something extra. Instead, you soaked up the sun's heat and told yourself you wanted to live forever. You got greedy for more life and now God's going to show you how wrong that bit of whimsy was.

You destroy a sign that reads: Closed to traffic. Now that you're on the pier, the boards under the Crown Vic sound like a hundred thundering hoofbeats.

Maybe the seatbelt will save you or maybe you'll be trapped in the car all the way to the bottom. A crazy thought crosses your mind: *My father will be waiting for me there*. But, of course, whatever might be left of Marco Diaz is amongst the deep coral off Florida's coast, somewhere around Surfside Beach if the currents didn't carry his remains farther out after the sharks were done.

The steel fence along the dock looks strong. At this speed, you figure it will part for you like balsa wood. Instead, the crash into the fence slows you and the car hits the edge of the dock like a pole vault. The nose goes down and the airbags deploy and you're cartwheeling. When you're airborne, your foot's still pressing the accelerator through the floor and the engine revs up, as if exhilarated at the sudden lack of friction.

Then things...slow...down. It's as if you're already underwater and trying to make sense of the world with eyes that perceive with hyperacuity. A spring in your brain is sprung and the works are turning at a quarter speed.

It feels like the roller coaster at Coney Island, the way your butt is lifted out of the seat a little, but this time you're upside down.

Now you're not.

Now you're upside down and now you aren't sure as you squeeze your eyes tight and throw up across the dashboard.

Ah, you were right side up, judging by the arc of the vomit. If not for the seatbelt, you'd break your neck when your head hit the roof.

Should you brace for impact with the water and risk breaking a leg? Or try to relax and imagine you are boneless and let the seatbelt do the work? The airbags are already deflating.

Before you can work out the right answer, the Crown Vic hits the water harder than you expect (and you expected the impact to feel like you were running into a brick wall).

Time and your brain slowed together when you were flying through the air. Now time speeds up, going way too fast to keep up. You aren't thinking anymore. You are not the smart ninja assassin you thought you'd finally become.

Dr. Fix is fucked and not in a good way.

RT READ THE DIVINE ASSASSIN'S PLAYBOOK FOR THE DATING TIPS A LA #ALBERTCAMUS

Your mother drowned. Your brother was chopped up by boat propellers and drowned. Your father drowned. That was a tough day off Surfside Beach.

You only lived because a murderous monster you called the Bug Man saved you for his torture chamber in a basement. Since you escaped the Bug Man and his evil mistress, Tia Marta, you've always suspected you were cursed. Despite all the bullets that habitually fly in your direction, you expected to die drowning at the bottom of the ocean.

Vicodin got you away from those dark thoughts for a while. Then you found vengeance was a higher high. As the car hits the water, you realize you probably should have stuck with Vicodin. As you begin to sink, you remember Dallas and Albert Camus.

You met Dallas in a military jail in Germany. You'd just punched a superior officer. Dallas was charged with stealing stuff from the PX to sell on the black market.

128

You'd killed a couple of people by then, but you didn't consider yourself a criminal. Not yet.

What impressed you most about Dallas was his overwhelming confidence. Prison didn't bother him. When he said, "Yes, sir," his emphasis was always on the *yes*. He dipped the *sir* so low, it's amazing he didn't get regular shit duty for insolence.

Dallas was a Private, six feet high and four feet wide. He got into the Army after 9/11 like you did, but he got in after the powers that be were desperate and loosened the physical fitness restrictions. He hadn't done a pushup since boot. Despite his lowly status, Dallas was supremely confident with women. He was everything you were not.

"I got into the Army for the uniform, man," he said. "Ladies dig the uniform. I'da gone with fireman, but they wouldn't take me."

As you waited for your court martial, Dallas schooled you on his pickup artistry. "Uniform's the first thing. After I get out of here, I'll still wear it. What's the Army gonna do? Keep me from buying stuff at military surplus stores? Shit, I shoulda thought of that before. I'da had me a chest full of fruit salad. The ladies love medals and ribbons. I could go to any house party and tell 'em how I won the war."

"We didn't win," you told him.

"Maybe so, but we'll never say so, am I right?"

"You're right."

"I'll tell you something else, man...I run the ladies several at a time. I never get caught."

You looked at him wearily and asked how he got caught stealing from the PX.

He shrugged and smiled and refused to say. He'd seen

you around the base with MP on your shoulder just days before so he wasn't going to talk about his case. You suspected he was stealing so he could finance all the dating he did with the local German women.

"I don't understand a word they say, but I sure like the way they say it," Dallas said. "They say what they want to say and I imagine the translation is all, 'Dallas, you're the best! Dallas don't leave me! Dallas, no man has ever made me feel this way!'"

"Maybe they're saying, 'Dallas, you sweat too much!'"

"Oh, man! Why'd you have to go and say that? I was about to give you the key to dating several women at a time with no problems. You're cut off. Suffer in silence, man."

Jail is boring. You said nothing for twenty minutes. It was Dallas who caved first. He laid out his dating strategy.

"Flirt with your eyes, man. That's the first thing."

"I thought the uniform was the first thing."

"*Sh.* I'm giving you the keys to the palace here. Next… where was I?"

"Flirting with your eyes. Even the lazy one?"

"My mother says that gives me character."

"Well, she would say that, right? What next?"

"Smile wide. That's the second thing. Chicks love a man who isn't the strong, silent type. That gets boring quick. I learned watching my older brothers. The shy ones don't date. Next is, be deep. You gotta keep it light and flirt, but you gotta throw some intelligence around. Talk about Albert Camus."

"Who?"

"That's it, right there. That's why you're in here for violence and I'm in here for spreading the love, man. You don't know Camus, you don't get laid. You got to know Camus. You don't get laid, some of that fluid pressure builds up and the next thing you know, you're taking a swing at your C.O. or something. You wanna be a swinger, you gotta be one with the Camus!"

"I'm listening."

"You gotta be sly. You slide it in that you're reading this book by Albert Camus. Suppose you're at a party and you give a lady the eye and she gives you a second glance. She don't know it, but you're already halfway to third base. You're looking sharp in your uniform."

"And if you aren't in uniform?"

"At least wear nice shoes. Sneakers are for dudes who hang out with other dudes in the gym. Don't be that guy. You dress nice, ladies notice."

"Okay. So she's given me a second look. Then what?"

"Lots of guys got lines and they're all bad. Don't put a line on a girl. You walk right up, eye contact, big smile and you introduce yourself. You get her name and you use it right away so you don't forget it."

"Is this a party girl you're talking to or are you trying to pass around business cards at a Toastmaster's meeting?"

Dallas laughed. "That's the pickup artist's problem. He's always looking for the shortcut. He don't know Camus. Besides, you wanna see somebody naked, she's gotta know you see her as a person. You wanna get to first base, you gotta let her know your mama churched you and raised you right."

"My mom's dead. We didn't do church."

"Hold off on the dead mom, man. If you aren't getting anywhere by the third date, you could try going dark. I don't recommend it. Dark ain't deep. It's just depressing.

I'm talking about first date action."

"Okay."

"So…where was I?"

"You were about to sell her aluminum siding and take her to church."

"Right. Handshake. Smile. You tell her, 'Hi, I'm Jesus Diaz. It's spelled like the Son of God but pronounced Hay-soose.'"

"Yeah, I'm kind of tired of that."

"Never mind. Tell her your Jose Conseco. Whatever. I'm getting to the good stuff."

"Sorry."

"You tell that party girl who's been hit on all night, 'What books are you reading?' And make sure you say books, not book. You're subtly communicating to her fine ass that you're intelligent but you also think she's intelligent. No pickup line does that."

"I do have a thing for women who wear glasses," you admit.

"All right, all right, roger-dodger. Now you have to let her know your lights are on. This is where you slide in the Camus."

"Is that a dick joke?"

"No. No, man. It's not."

"Oh."

"Can I continue?"

"Sure."

"You tell her you're blown away by this Algerian philosopher you been reading. You say, 'People think he was an existentialist, but he was actually an absurdist.'" Dallas clapped his hands and showed his palms like he'd just performed a startling magic trick.

You stared at him for a moment. "I'm going to have a nap now."

"You're *missing* it, man! Camus wrote these cool ass stories about how he's gotta go to his mother's funeral and he kills a dude."

"Sounds depressing. I thought down wasn't the same as deep?"

"Context for your play, Jesus. It's all about context. She's thinking you're a deep, sensitive kind of guy and then you add the magic spell. You tell her how fascinating Camus was because he was all for personal and *sexual* freedom. You drop that on her and then you can get with the flirty and the double innuendos."

"Double entendres?"

"Yeah. Whatever. French shit's good, too."

"This works? It can't. You don't even understand any German!" You laid back on your bunk and closed your eyes.

"No, man. This is for running your game when we get out of here and head back home."

"So, here, you're just going to German prostitutes."

"Man, I'm trying to pass the time and giving you gold and here you come, all about judgment and shit."

"Fine. You done?"

"You're being rude, but I'm going to give you the secret formula that lets you run several ladies at a time without one of them waking you up one morning by cutting your dick off."

You sat up and nodded. "I do want to know how to avoid that."

"When you're all flirty and she's all flirty and you both know it's going somewhere? You tell her, 'It is a fucking tragedy I have a girlfriend.'"

"*What?*"

"Yeah. I know, right?"

"You're insane."

"No, no, man. Now she knows you got value. If you're single, there's something wrong. You're communicating to her that she's a fantasy and you're already proven and tested your own self."

"I'm going to sleep. Some girl is going to kill you."

"Lemme finish. I haven't laid the magic words on her yet. You make like you're about to go. You begin with a goodbye handshake, but then you kiss the back of her hand, like you can't help yourself. Then you say, 'You are such a beautiful person...such a *sexy* woman...my God, what fun we could have had if you only could keep a secret... *Ta-da!*'"

"Ta-da? What then?"

"Then you walk away."

"I walk away?"

"You walk away." Dallas smiles. "She'll follow you out to your car. Don't chase women, man. Let them chase you. You find one you like, you let 'em catch you."

"This is your dating strategy?"

"Absolutely. Do that five times a night and you never go home alone. One of five girls will follow you out to your car. You're letting her take the responsibility of being the predator for a change. You're just a little rabbit who can't help himself in the face of her stunning beauty."

"What about the other four girls who laugh in your face?"

"They aren't smart enough for you. Any girl gets with me, she's gotta be down with the Camus and personal and sexual freedom. You want a big life after we get out of here? Read some Camus."

"I still think somebody's going to cut your dick off."

"Not before I make full use of it," Dallas said. His belly convulsed in ripples as he giggled.

As you sink into the Pacific, that memory of Dallas sitting in the corner of a cell, shirtless, his torso convulsing with each high giggle, comes back to you.

Why now? Because you're about to drown. Your life is about to be cut short and you have not made full use of it.

RT HOW NOT TO ESCAPE DROWNING IN A CAR. @ASSASSINSPLAYBK

Exhibit 1 in your diary of a death by drowning in a car: The seatbelt is way too hard to figure out.

Your hands shake and your feet are cold. You try to slow your breathing because smart ninjas don't die by drowning. Your body doesn't want to cooperate with your orders. Though the autopsy report will say death by drowning, it should read: Death by the intersection of Panic and Stupid.

Exhibit 2: Your feet are already wet and you still aren't out of that seatbelt. Is the buckle jammed or are your fingers just numb, cold and dumb as all the blood rushes to your core? You glance in the rearview mirror. The face you barely recognize looks frantic, wild-eyed and white with shock.

Exhibit 3: You should have tried to open the door immediately, while there were only a few inches at the bottom of the door. Did you float for long while you sat in the driver's seat, dazed, confused and staring ahead at the Pacific's expanse stretching to Japan? You'll never see

Japan, now, bonehead.

Exhibit 4: You finally figure out the deep intricacies of the seatbelt buckle and free yourself. You push at the door, but the water's already up to the window. You should be saving your strength for the nosedive to the bottom. You're plunging into darkness. How far a drop is it to the bottom? Maybe you should have kept that seatbelt on. Damn.

Exhibit 5: When the Pacific closes over the car, instinctively, you duck. Clearly, your instincts suck. Plus, that happened a minute ago but you're only remembering it now. Nothing makes sense. Time is messed up.

Exhibit 6: You're scrambling to get the seatbelt back on when the front bumper hits the bottom with a muted crash, and the car goes over unevenly, like it's hit sand and rock and silt. You had pictured a soft landing on all four tires. Instead, the bang rattles your teeth and you're plunged into the darkness of a dust cloud that blots out the headlights. Cold water climbs to your neck, shaking you further and jangling every nerve.

Exhibit 7: The water inside and outside should equalize the pressure on the door. You push hard. The door doesn't budge. The impact with the fence or with the Pacific's bottom must have jammed the doors shut. When you dig out your pen light, you discover your door is locked. The lock on a new Crown Vic should pop even if it is locked. This is an old Crown Vic. You should have listened when Skunk carried on about his alterations to his precious ride. Instead, you nodded politely and tuned out. You're losing time.

Exhibit 8: The lights are out, but for some reason you can't fathom, you're wasting more time trying the electric windows. You want to take a deep breath to calm down, but the cabin is quickly filling with water. The cold slap in your face says you don't have the luxury of the time it takes to be Zen about your looming demise.

Exhibit 9: You close your eyes and Lily pops up. You thought you were going to marry her. You've thought you were going to marry several women, but you walked away from them. Lily's the one who walked away from you. Lily's saying something. She looks angry. Lily often looked angry but no less beautiful. Then you get it. She's screaming, "You don't have time for this! Wake up, Jesus. *Resurrect, bitch!*"

It's time to be Batman, if Batman packed a SIG Sauer P220. You take a last breath, pull your pistol and fire out the window. The driver's side window splinters and the rest of the Pacific runs in to the roof.

The rear tires aren't down, either because you're tipped on the ocean floor or because there's an air bubble back there. There's supposed to be. You've got an SAS manual and they always sound sure about these things. However, the SAS manual is about escaping a submerged vehicle. They didn't have a chapter devoted to escaping the police after escaping a submerged vehicle.

Your father taught you how to swim in Cuba, but you haven't been in the ocean, or even a pool with water in it, since you were a kid. Nearly drowning and the subsequent kidnapping in Florida messed up your plans for more beach-going fun. You swore you'd never get in the water again. You pull yourself through the window and head back toward the pier, into the teeth of your pursuers. That still feels cozier than the trap of an underwater metal tomb.

You break the surface and cling to the bottom of the

pier, gasping. You're cold, but the air tastes sweet. A police helicopter comes into view and you dive again, heading around the pier. It's a long swim back to the pilings underneath the amusement park.

Somewhere in the long swim underwater, you lose your Tanini Crisci shoes. You're exhausted, but memories drive you on. The image of your drowning father chases you to shore.

Losing $1,200 shoes puts things in perspective. Some guys would get spiritual about escaping near-death. A lot of men would take this perilous misadventure as a sign to disappear to Mexico and start a quiet life of charity, peace and contemplation. But you aren't going to start chewing granola, go barefoot and become a vegan now.

The attack on Chill makes you want to kill Hank Reles very much, of course. Losing those expensive shoes makes you want to kill him, but to do the job slower.

And what those men did to Ginger in Oswald's secret slave room? That makes you think an Apocalypse would be a peachy idea right about now. If that's what the world is underneath, why live?

RT HOW TO EQUIP A SURVEILLANCE VAN. @ASSASSINPLAYBK

When you reach the shore and hide under the pier, there's still a better than even chance that the police chopper will spot you. However, they're focusing on where you went, not where you are. The helicopter hovers a few feet above the water drilling deep with their searchlight. Reles pulls to the edge of the pier first and stands there, staring at the water, hands in his pockets, probably smirking.

The CHP cruiser screeches to a stop behind him. That hero doesn't hesitate to pull off his shoes, holster, belt and radio gear. The cop slams his stuff on the hood of his car and jumps into the Pacific, intent on saving you.

You forgot. They aren't all bad. You were one of them once. Okay…so don't blow up the world. A few are worth saving.

You creep away before the forces for earthly justice expand their search and set up a perimeter.

You walk away, then you run, then you walk, alternating between inconspicuous and terrified. Finally, you rest and shiver under a table at the International Chess Park. It's not really a park. There isn't any grass. It's just a place people come to play chess with strangers.

The irony isn't lost on you. You've had three run-ins with Detective Hank Reles. At the coffee shop he saw through your play too easily. In Legs Gabrielle's dry pool, you played him to a draw. As car chases go, he beat you bad. You're alive and not in custody, but that was mostly dumb luck.

Before dawn, you pull yourself up and make your way toward the rendezvous point. It's two miles. The police could pick you up at any time. You hope Sgt. Billy remembered to bring the surveillance van. You won't relax until you're safely hidden behind those tinted windows and blackout curtains. If you'd had time to plan ahead, you would have asked for a towel, a change of clothes and shoes. A different face, a fresh name and a new life would be good, too. Something safe, possibly in advertising.

Chill keeps a white panel surveillance van in a garage not far from his office. Behind its tinted windows are three pieces of gear: low-light, very low light and zoom cameras. Chill paid close to $10,000 just for the cameras. There's also a periscope, a computer, remote joysticks to control the cameras from a custom console and audio and video recording equipment. It looks like any other commercial van on the street except for the dual antennae, but that's only a tip off to people who look closely.

Unlike a typical surveillance van, Chill also invested in commercial camouflage. Several different magnetic signs can plaster the sides of the vehicle. Chill's crew calls it the bakery wagon because, most of the time, the sign across the hood and rear reads: *Grace's Baking.*

Grace's Baking is a tribute to Chill's mother, Grace Gillie. Down the side, the slogan reads in bright yellow letters: *Try our donuts! The burnt ones are free!* Chill says the company name is a subtle nod to Grace's marijuana habit. The slogan acknowledges that his mom's cooking sucked.

The Rose Cafe and Market opens at 7 a.m. You arrive there by 7:15. Sgt. Billy is waiting for you in the van, chewing Eggs Scandia. That's poached eggs on a croissant with lox. He's got one for you, too. You're grateful and starving.

Sgt. Billy waits until you're seated, hands you the food and a little plastic fork. The coffee is still hot. You take a deep breath and get comfortable in your chair. It's a race to see if you can finish breakfast before you fall asleep. But you can't eat or sleep. You can only cry because Billy tells you Chill, your boss and friend, is dead.

RT HOW NOT TO MEET A CELEBRITY. @ASSASSINSPLAYBK

Sgt. Billy delivers you safely home, such as it is. The ceiling leaks when it rains and the wood is rotting around you. When your business is done in L.A., you'll have to move on. Hollywood will never be the same without Chill. Without Chill, who will save you from yourself?

From the moment you met Chillie Gillie in Chicago, he showed you a way out of the thug life. Like you, he'd done things of which he was not proud. He'd put the bad stuff behind him and gave you a job and a future. Chill took you in and encouraged you to use your talents more cleverly.

Sgt. Billy hands you a cappuccino. The espresso machine, the laptops and the weaponry are the only fancy bits of tech in this dump. You've got a hotplate for a stove and a tiny fridge for the cream. Your bed is a futon thrown on the floor.

Sgt. Billy used to live on the streets of Chicago so this is a step up for him. For you? The hope Chill offered was what kept you here. The California sunshine elevated your mood. Now? You might need to hit the anti-depressants again. And by "anti-depressants" you mean seek an even more terrible vengeance against Reles and his crew.

"How you doin', Chief?"

"Okay. Did you call Skunk?"

"Yeah. He reported his car stolen. The cops haven't called him yet, but he knows the deal." The old man sighs. "I never thought Chill would go before me. My heart works at forty percent and I'm so creaky in the morning. Have to get up six times in the night to piss. Prostate's prolly the size of a softball. And Chill was such a tough son of a bitch."

He was. After he was stabbed in Chicago, he pulled himself out of a hospital bed early so he could get back to his life in Hollywood.

"You're awfully quiet, Ace. Longest time I've heard you go without crackin' off a joke. I don't get your jokes all the time, but — "

"I'm thinking of something Chill said to me, Billy. He said I don't have to pull my pistol out every time. He asked me to use a little finesse and stay righteous."

"Chill was smarter than you."

"Yeah."

"We're in a crazy business, Jesus. We see pretty people up on a screen forty feet high, the nuts get jealous or they think they know 'em or own 'em. It's just a matter of time before somebody kills or captures the idols they worship."

A few people do get insane about celebs, but they aren't all as crazy as Detective Hank Reles is about Legs Gabrielle. You've definitely felt star struck, too. You met Joe Rogan in a Whole Foods parking lot once and you still curse yourself and burn with embarrassment at the memory.

You couldn't seem to stop yourself from quizzing Rogan about his old sitcom, *News Radio*. The episode in which the cast bid a fond farewell to comedian Phil Hartman was the only episode of a television show that made you cry. Funny and loveable, Hartman was murdered in his sleep.

Murdered while helpless. That's your second biggest fear, next to drowning.

"Chill was proud of you most when you held back a little, Jesus. His favorite was the game show case." Sgt. Billy's cackle ends in a cough and a wheeze.

Despite everything, you allow a small smile. In the case of the Tank versus the game show host, Chill approved your play. A powerlifter named Chris Gardenia ran a gym in Pasadena. He shot steroids into his ass so heavily, he was known to police as a habitual 'roid rager and road rager. ("Known to police" is a cop euphemism for "an asshole we can't seem to keep in jail for long.")

His fellow gym rats called him Tank because of his penchant for getting into fights with bouncers. His move was to run at club security from behind and slam them into walls. Then the floor. The guy had an unhealthy obsession with moving heavy shit up and down in the form of barbells. He was such a hard juicer that the steroids had swollen his jaw east and west, much like Reles. Tank also had an obsession with a top game show host.

Think of the top game show hosts. The one that first comes to mind was Tank's intended victim. Tank Gardenia — all muscle, obsessive personality and zero charm — was determined to become best friends with said game show host, even if it meant doing something stupid. Doing something stupid is usually what's required for an ordinary mortal/stalker to meet a celeb. However, few stalkers of your experience are smart enough to get on a game show (even the most moronic game shows.)

Tank's solution was to follow the talk show host from a taping at the studio. When the host backed out of a Trader Joe's parking space, the stalker saw his chance. Tank shot forward in his Camaro — yes, of course, it was a fucking Camaro — and made sure the celebrity backed into him. One dented fender later, Tank had the game show host's insurance information, including the celeb's address and phone number.

This minor accident did not blossom into the game show guy and Captain Road Rage becoming besties forever. The friendly phone calls imploring the celeb to train with Tank began. Those phone calls soon got less friendly. Next, Tank demanded the host take him to dinner at Melisse.

"If you don't want to meet with me for dinner, take me to lunch and hang out, instead," Tank said. "I'll show you what you should be eating."

The host politely declined.

"I understand. But you'll understand if I do something crazy with your address. I could put it up on the net, for instance. So if I were you, I'd get with my program and forget about calling the police or getting a restraining order. You do that, maybe I'll bang your girlfriend or shoot your dog. I'm trying to be nice, here, but you don't seem to want to listen to reason. I'm not like your regular fans, bro. I'm your super fan. I'm looking out for you!"

The host gave Tank the name and number of his

lawyer for any further inquiries about fixing his car. Game show guy hung up and changed his number and tried to forget the crazed muscle man.

Then a shitty old Camaro with a dent in its front fender started sliding by his front gate each night. Game show guy spent more money on his security system and put another lock on his bedroom door. The Camaro came back, three or four nights a week at odd times, driving slow as the driver laid on the horn.

When Tank appeared at the dog park and held the host's little pug in his massive hands, smiling and petting the animal, the game show host finally got really scared.

Sitting safe in Chill's office, game show guy shook as he told about the look on the steroid freak's face.

"Tank said, 'I own you. You think you're so high and mighty and rich and famous, but backing into my car is all it takes for me to be your lord and master. It's so easy. I know where you live. I know who your friends are. I know where your mom lives. What are you going to do? Nothing. Nothing but what I tell you.'"

Game show guy promised to take Tank to lunch. Then he hurried away with his little dog and ran to Chill. Tank's target didn't need a restraining order or more police patrols in his neighborhood. He called the professionals because he needed a smart ninja on his side.

RT HOW NOT TO KILL A STALKER. @ASSASSINSPLAYBK

"Don't kill the Tank," Chill said.

"He needs it," you said.

"Find another way."

"What if we don't call it a shooting? How about...lead poisoning at 1,150 feet per second?"

"How about no?"

"But one trigger pull is so easy."

"Think about it longer. Be imaginative," Chill said.

You didn't have to destroy Tank's computer and set fire to his house. He'd left his computer on and his browser open when he went off to work. It would have been fun to get into Tank's bank account and make some bank transfers to charity. However, you didn't have those passwords.

Fortunately, Tank left the file on the computer's desktop with all the information he'd gathered on Chill's client. It wasn't just the game show host that Tank obsessed over. Tank had a list of targets. As you scanned the names, you realized he had a stalker file on the entire cast of *Family*

Ties. You tossed that in the computer's trash can, too, and erased it.

To take out Tank, you needed something strong. You searched his apartment. The rich have safes for money, jewels and guns. The poor keep their cash, porn and guns under the mattress. The middle class always keep their valuables in the sock drawer. Tank had a spare credit card hidden in his sock drawer in the bedroom. You spent half an hour downloading child porn to Tank's computer using his credit card.

There are, of course, too many sex offenders in the world for the police to get to in a timely manner. It was necessary to get the cops' attention. You printed some labels.

You checked in with Sgt. Billy. Your elderly sidekick was in the donut van, inches from Tank's back bumper in a traffic jam on the Glendale Freeway. Plenty of time.

You emailed Tank's boss and, pretending to be Tank, announced that you were quitting immediately because you were "sick of dealing with his shit."

You wrote that Tank had taken a copy of all the gym's account information. You wrote that data would be useful for when he opened his own gym. You railed on quite a bit — spewing hatred, curses and racial epithets on Tank's behalf.

You implied that if you didn't cool off over the weekend, you might return to work and "shoot the whole gym in the goddamn face."

Workplace shootings almost always involve a disgruntled employee facing Monday morning. You added a link to an old video of the Boomtown Rats singing about a school shooting. *I don't like Mondays.* Good song, and sure to earn Tank a no-knock entry from SWAT.

You set the email so it wouldn't send until Tank was home so he'd have no deniability. As strained as police forces are — and strained they must be since they haven't caught you, yet — two more stops were in order.

At a sleazy corner store where most of the security cameras were obvious fakes, you loaded up on the most explicit and imaginative porn you can find in paper: Gay, straight and fetish. You had no idea there were still so many varieties of these kinds of magazines. Really poor perves can't afford computers, so there must still be a market for the paper variety of porn.

The magazines are strangely specific: whole magazines devoted to one subject, like footjob cuckolding. This is the sort of lunacy the Internet was built for. Who still buys this stuff unless they're on a mission to get rid of a stalker?

To whit, your next stop is the nearest library. In the car, you stick the labels on each of the magazines. Each label reads the same:

This generous donation of literature made possible by Chris Gardenia. Train with me at my gym so you look this good naked, too!

As you browse the library shelves, you slip the magazines at random intervals among the books in the Religion section.

The police will get several irate calls from elderly library patrons and, of course, Tank's boss, in short order. The boss will want to retrieve the information on Tank's computer, which, of course, isn't there. Though that beef is a civil matter, the added boost of an anonymous tip from an anguished librarian should get a warrant to cart off his computer.

In your call to the tip line, you will complain that a man matching Tank's unique description wanted to take naked pictures of your son. You followed him from the elementary school down the street to Tank's address. That will surely light a fire under the asses of local law enforcement. Tank's tiny mind will be fully occupied with other pursuits besides threatening famous game show hosts. There will be no more midnight runs past his favorite game show host's house.

You also added Tank's home address to the labels, in case some devout NRA-loving churchgoer wants to have a productive chat with Tank about putting all-anal porn in amongst the old issues of *Guns & Ammo*.

Sgt. Billy rouses you from your warm reverie. "Do you think you may have overdone it on that job, Jesus? Even though you didn't shoot anybody?"

"The cops are overworked and there are too many bad guys to catch. They need all our support and encouragement."

"When will Tank get out of jail, anyway?"

"He'll be away so long, when he comes out he'll no longer be 'known to police.'"

"So…what's next for us? Now that the boss has passed on?"

"Chill didn't pass on, Billy. He died of a brain hemorrhage after Reles fractured his skull."

Sgt. Billy stares at you for a moment more. "You want to use your imagination again, don't you?"

You shrug. "Mostly I just want to shoot Hank Reles and Detective Mueller in the face. But maybe I can come up with something more imaginative. With Chill's death, I feel the need to make a statement. Execution is too easy."

"Reles and Mueller...they're still *cops*, Jesus. Killing's easy. Walking away...well, running away, is hard."

"Chill's not here. No holding back now."

"They'll kill you. If not them, their buddies. These are sick in the head bastards."

You lie back on your futon and stare up at the water stained boards in the rotting ceiling. "That's okay. I gotta be me."

When you open your eyes, Sgt. Billy is shaking you awake. Skunk stands in the doorway. Legs Gabrielle and Sugar Cane stand with him. Legs can't stop crying.

RT SIDEKICKS NEED EMERGENCY CODE WORDS SO THEY KNOW WHEN TO PANIC. @ASSASSINSPLAYBK

You pull yourself to your feet stiffly. You put a hand out to Skunk. "Sorry about your car, man."

Skunk startles you by pulling you into a hug. His eyes are wet. "I'm just so sorry about Chill. That's all I can think about. Insurance will take care of the car. Money can't bring back a downed soldier. Chill was the best of us. They must have bushwhacked him, Fix."

Your gaze slides to the ladies. Legs has been crying. Sugar looks scared, but the woman you rescued from Oswald's cage looks better than when you saw her last. Evidently, Sugar kept your true identity to herself, but her presence still screws up operational security. "Sergeant, could you go down to the bodega and get us some more cream for coffee? Soy, this time, please? That'd be good for us."

Sgt. Billy nods and dips his head to the women on his way out. He knows that if you ask for soy, he's on recon duty.

Skunk whispers in your ear. "Sorry to take them to your lair, man. Miss Gabrielle insisted. She and Chill go way back. Berb and the Samoan weren't available and I couldn't leave them both alone."

"It's...not optimum, but it's fine." You live in a hovel with a futon on a bare wood floor. It's not the image your Armani suits project when you're out in the world. Your poverty is embarrassing. Worse, you're embarrassed that they know you're embarrassed. Letting people see you as you are gives up too much power.

You take a deep breath and focus on Skunk. "I didn't expect to see Sugar again."

"I dropped her off at the hospital as ordered."

"Sugar came to me," Legs says. "I heard what happened to Oswald. Sugar told me enough about her kidnapping...about Ginger. We all know he deserved what he got."

"Legs took me in," Sugar says. "I didn't know where else to go. I can identify these men. What if they come after me?"

You nod. "My fault. I should have told you how to disappear. Too pressed for time to think straight, I guess."

Skunk pipes up. "Sugar said you told her to keep me out of this. I appreciate it, Fix, but this is Chill we're talking about now. You need me for anything? I'm down, dog."

You can't help but smile. Skunk's a solid dude, but somebody should stay pure. "The first night I met Chill," you reply, "we came to an agreement. I'd take care of the dirty tricks and morally ambiguous stuff. He'd take care of things on his end. 'I don't know and I don't want to know,' was Chill's official policy."

"I can work unofficially on this one," Skunk says.

You shake your head. "Eventually, Chill and I worked it out so I kept him informed on cases on a need-to-know basis. Let's keep that approach with you, man. Take care of the funeral and deal with questions from 5-0. I'll get my hands dirty. Chill would want to keep you clean. Somebody's got to be the face of the company now. That's you."

You nod to Legs. "Exactly how far do you go back with Chill?"

"I gave him his first bodyguard job when he quit trying to be an actor. Way back."

"Like family," you say.

She nods. Her jaw is tight. She's not just sad. She's furious.

"Skunk, what are you driving now?" you ask.

"Caddy. Rental."

"Could you go check out the seats? Make sure they're comfortable. The ladies and I need to have a quick chat upstairs."

You need to make sure neither of them will lose their nerve and call in the police or the FBI. You hate depending on strangers, but for you to do your job, you have to make sure they can keep their mouths shut. If Legs and Sugar come to their senses and fall back into acting like ordinary, good citizens, you're dead before you can even begin your campaign of vengeance.

RT SERIOUSLY CONSIDER RUNNING AWAY. LIVE LONGER. @ASSASSINSPLAYBK

You show Sugar and Legs the stairs to the roof. The view from your dreary little piece of Los Angeles shows busy streets and wandering homeless people. The sun shines as if it doesn't care that Charles "Chill" Gillie is dead. People go about their business as if his murder doesn't matter. If the universe had a face, you'd punch it.

"You okay?" Legs asks.

"Pretty broken up, but I'm finding my rage."

"Why did Reles kill Chill?"

"Because he would have stood in the way of getting to you." The look on her face tells you that wasn't diplomatic enough. Dealing with clients and being charming is Chill's job...*was* Chill's job.

"Why don't you just leave town?" The way Sugar says it, it's more of a statement than a question. "You can't win against Reles and Mueller. Just run. We should all get away."

"Let me worry about that. I still don't know anything

about Bekhti. What can you tell me about him?"

"I heard Mueller call him Gaston. He likes to watch. He finds the girls, too. He watched Ginger die. Reles did it. Mueller recorded it. He joked about how he had often photographed crime scenes, but never before the fact."

"Where did Bekhti find you?"

"Craigslist."

"And?"

"He was a generous older man."

"What was the ad?"

"Searching for submissives into BDSM."

"If you're so submissive, how come I had to drag the information out of you?"

"Hey!" Legs says sharply.

Sugar avoids your gaze, her eyes fixed on the big, dead rooftop air conditioning unit that sits over your flop. "I'm not proud," she says. "Ginger was a friend. I brought her in. We both needed the money."

"Don't we all?" As soon as you say it, you realize you're standing next to someone for whom money is not a problem. "You should get out of town, Legs. I know it's not convenient, but — "

"You're not going anywhere, right?"

"Nope."

"You're going to do something. For Chill?"

"In his memory, yes. I feel like I have to."

"Sugar's right. We should run."

"He won't," Sugar says. "I've seen his scars." She begins to cry. She runs at you. Her embrace begins as a hug. Then she's pulling your shirt off.

You stand in the presence of two women in broad daylight. They stare at your torso. Legs's mouth drops open. Your chest and stomach are a road map of scars. Crosses.

Sugar stands close, your shirt forgotten in her hand. "Who did this to you?"

"People. Two of them. I was a kid."

"That's why you won't run," Sugar says. She reaches out tentatively and caresses your chest where the worst scar lies.

It's in the shape of a cross, too, but thicker than the others. When you insisted on using your name, Tia Marta tried to make you forget your name is Jesus. She heated a crucifix in fire and hung it around your neck. Tia Marta branded you. She thought that was an ironic joke.

Sugar's voice is barely above a whisper. "You won't try to get away from Reles or Mueller or Bekhti. You'll come right at them because, like me, you are a glutton for punishment."

You grab Sugar's hand and push it away, burning in embarrassment at being exposed like this. You've spent most of your adult life having sex with your clothes on, trying to avoid conversations like this. "I am not a glutton for punishment."

Sugar shrugs. "Sure looks like it."

"Every time I talked back, they'd punish me. I thought they would kill me dozens of times over. I kept talking back until I couldn't talk anymore. Then it got worse."

You turn your naked back to the women. They gasp in unison. "If I tried to escape, they'd burn me with the edge of an iron."

"It...it looks like...wings!" Sugar says.

"Yes. Another of Tia Marta's little jokes. She said if I kept trying to defy them, she would give me wings before

158

she killed me."

"It's beautiful," Sugar said. "So…symmetrical."

"No!" You and Legs say it at the same time.

You twist and grab the shirt from Sugar's hand. "It's not beautiful, Sugar. My point is, I'm not a glutton for punishment. Like you and Ginger, I was a victim. Now I'm a glutton for justice."

You walk to the edge of the roof and pull your shirt on, covering up quickly and buttoning up slow so you give yourself time to calm down.

"I'm sorry for what happened to you," Legs says. "I understand…I'm glad you aren't walking away from this."

You hang your head. "I'll finish it."

Below you is a dark blue van parked on the far side of the street. It looks like any other commercial van, except for the dual antennae. You squint and look closer. It has a periscope. Its telescopic microphone is pointed at you.

It's not LAPD. If it were, they'd be coming through the door and shooting you already.

It's not the Spanish mob. They'd wait for you to go down to the bodega, pull you into a van and shoot you in the back of the head. It's not your one-time friend, Big Denny De Molina. If he knew where you were, he'd come straight from LAX to shoot you in the face.

It's probably the FBI, but your imagination runs wild. It could even be the CIA for all you know. The Company would prioritize gathering information above busting you. First they gather data. Then they use you. When they're done with guys like you, you don't see the inside of a court. They might put a hood over your head and you'd wake up at a black site naked and primed for torture. Best case scenario, they simply kill you.

Chill warned you that you couldn't walk away with a shipment of Russian TM40 mines and expect no one to come looking of them. They won't have to look far to find the explosives.

Whatever spy agency it is, you're in Big Brother's sights and in the open. Time to knot your tie nonchalantly, casually step out of sight and run and run and run.

RT CLEAN GETAWAYS ARE DIFFICULT. @ASSASSINSPLAYBK

You meet Billy on the stairs and you both whisper "Feds!" at the same moment.

"Take the ladies out the back, through the restaurant. If it looks clear, get them in the van. Take off the bakery signs, change the plates and get out the magnetic signs for the plumbing business." (*Gill's Plumbing. We lay pipe and open your drain!*)

"How will I know if it looks clear?"

"You'll only know for sure when you get away. They've got nothing on you anyway, so don't sweat it."

"What about you?"

You give the old man a hug. "I'll be okay, Mother."

"But what about your cache — "

"Go. We're walking away from it. When I have an assignment for you, I'll call. You know where I'll be until then."

He was a soldier. Heart attacks and age don't change a thing. Sgt. Billy still follows orders. He knows better than to tell you to stay safe. Instead, when he tosses you a glance over his shoulder, he says, "Jesus? Win."

You can't recall ever achieving an unqualified victory. Winning is a tall order.

Legs wishes you good luck and hurries after Billy. Sugar pauses at the door and blows you a kiss. "Bye, sweetie!"

"Bye."

She disappears down the stairs.

Well...that's a lonely feeling. You used to crave being alone. All you wanted was for the world to leave you alone. Too bad you still don't feel that way because, if this play goes wrong, at best you're going to spend a lot of time in a SHU. Though "Segregated Housing Unit" sounds awfully fancy for getting thrown in Solitary when the your cell will be nothing more than a small, dark hole.

You click your comm rig twice and Skunk rolls up to your door a moment later. As you exit the door, you're carrying as many Armani suits as you can, high and on their hangers, still in their plastic sheaths from the dry cleaners.

You've already changed into a dark blue suit, almost identical to that of Skunk. Your hands shook as you hurried to change, wondering if the Alphabet Agency would burst through the door at any moment.

You give Skunk the nod to pop the trunk but you open the Caddy's back door and slip in the back seat. The surveillance van is down the block a bit on the other side of the street. You wait for a truck to rumble by. Skunk goes back to close the trunk and you slip back out of the Caddy, head down until you're back in Big in Japan.

Skunk stands in the street at the driver's door and appears to be having an animated conversation. Talking to an empty back seat full of your suits would be funny if your freedom wasn't on the line. He makes a gesture of exasperation, really selling it, and jumps in the Caddy. Then he peels out.

The surveillance van does not move. However, two identical cars pull out to follow him. As they pass your window, you think, "Goodbye, Powers Without Judgment."

You turn to find Agent John Smith from Elizabeth, New Jersey staring at you from his seat, a half-eaten bento box of unagi in front of him. Nobody who wants to eat that much eel can be a good guy. You haven't seen Smith since New York. He's sweating through a blue Oxford shirt. His 9 mm is pointed at your chest.

You smile. "Hello, Power Without Judgment."

"Jesus Diaz AKA Dr. JD Fix."

"Yup. So, that was an FBI van watching me. I hope you got my good side. I've got a great ass. You should see me twerk on Instagram."

"I told them you'd come downstairs for some sushi eventually. Keep your hands where I can see them, don't move and sit down."

"Okay. Shall I not move first? Or should I sit and then not move?"

He directs you to your seat with the gun. The restaurant is empty except for the cook and one waiter and he's fled to the kitchen.

"Can I have some of your sushi? I'm not sure what the food is like at Gitmo. I understand it's often what they can blend up and force feed you."

"Shut up."

"Okay."

"I have two messages for you. The first is from Big

Denny."

"How is he?"

"He's feeling better. Losing weight. Barbara's getting him to eat organic and they're into green juicing."

"Nice. They married yet?"

"Barbara wants to wait a while longer before walking down the aisle again. Since you killed Jimmy...guess she doesn't wanna look like the merry widow."

He's not calling you in. He doesn't even have his earbud in. John Smith is a pretty good sport considering that the last time you saw him you made fun of his name and screwed up his assignment. You took over his observation post in a post office so your ex-girlfriend could get away with a lot of money.

Every good deed, mistake and misstep ties itself to the next until you've got enough trouble to hang yourself.

RT THINGS GO EASIER IF YOU MAKE
WEAK ENEMIES. @ASSASSINSPLAYBK

"**D**id you get in trouble?" you ask. "After New York? Demoted? Did they make fun of you, I mean besides for your stupid white guy name? When I took your gun and radio, did the other agents razz you a bit? Make you leave meetings for sandwiches and coffee? I guess every office is like that. I dunno. I never really worked in an office."

He doesn't look eager to exchange pleasantries. "My career advancement options would have been limited, but since I'm the only FBI agent who can positively ID you in person, I got assigned to track down my favorite domestic terrorist."

"Dude! Please! Not everybody who blows shit up is a terrorist. Is that your disdain face? That looks like it must be your disdain face."

"Mr. Diaz, we live in a country with Ag Gag laws. If a hippie who tries to take pictures at a slaughterhouse can be classified as a terrorist, you certainly are a terrorist."

"Denny must be paying you so goddamn much money, it hurts! What's the plan? If Denny's paying you to take

165

me somewhere for a long, drawn out torture session, pull the trigger now. I've been tortured enough in my life. Actually, if you plan to arrest me, I'll reach for my SIG right now and we can finish — "

"Shut up."

You sigh. "Okay."

"Big Denny says hello and he says keep doing what you're doing. You're on the right track."

"What?"

"You have a common enemy, apparently. Big Denny wants you to do what you do."

You take a deeper breath. Your heart rate begins to slow. Agent Smith is not going to shoot you. However, you've been set up for the long con. "How did you pick up my trail again, exactly?"

He smirks. "Denny's a big wheel now. He's got reach."

"Denny's got money mojo now, sure, but enough to get you to turn a blind eye?"

"I'm not turning a blind eye for long, Mr. Diaz. Nobody's got that much money. You threatened my family."

"I didn't mean it, John."

"Felt like it."

"Sorry, but believing that I would kill your family was kind of key to the bit, right? How would it have gone down if you hadn't taken me seriously?"

"You aren't getting away again, Jesus. We've got you dialed in. You aren't leaving LA. Satellites. Surveillance. Pictures. Meta-data. Data. Shoe size. We know all your associates. I even have a photo of you kissing Legs Gabrielle. That won't bode well for her career, palling around with known terrorists."

166

"One, leave her out of it. Two, you're quoting Sarah Palin and 'palling around with terrorists' didn't stop Obama's election. Besides which, if the President knew what I did for him in Chicago, I'd get a pardon."

"Chicago. Thanks for the confirmation. Do you have to leave a trail of blown up houses *everywhere* you go?"

"It's a bad habit. I'm trying to quit."

"You aren't hearing me, Jesus. I *own* you."

"That's what all stalkers say. So I go ahead with my mission — "

"Whatever you have planned, I don't want to know."

"I get that a lot. What happens when I'm done?"

Smith smiles ear to ear. "Well, then I get to shoot you, of course. Denny's not paying me to be a traitor, you piece of shit. He's paying me to wait a few days before I'm declared a hero."

He's startled when you push your chair back and stand. "Well, you know what they say. When you work by the hour, slow the fuck down. Let's revisit this when I'm done, okay? Did Denny mention which common enemy I'm taking out for him?"

"You were both enforcers for The Machine, right? Betcha you guys made lots of enemies together."

"I think Big Denny might have pointed an old enemy my way hoping I'd kill or be killed, am I right?"

"Jesus?" Smith raises his pistol, points it at your crotch and yells, "Bang!"

You jump back and come very close to shitting your pants and peeing at the same time. "That's just mean, man."

"That was the second message. From me to you, bitch."

You won't give him the satisfaction of watching you run

away so you walk fast and fight to keep the pace below a scurry. Your heart doesn't stop hammering in your chest until you're two blocks away. Yes, that was definitely Smith's disdain face. He intends to shoot you, but only if you give him one chance.

Mental note: Don't do that.

RT DRESS LIKE BRUCE LEE WHENEVER POSSIBLE. @ASSASSINSPLAYBK

Your backup hideout is a storage facility in West Carson. It's not much more comfortable than the dump over Big in Japan. There's no working air conditioner in either location. You're back to sleeping on the floor so it feels pretty much the same.

You need to find the mystery man, Gaston Bekhti. If you had more manpower, you'd take them all down at once. Maybe there's a way to do that by going after the trio's weakest point.

Since the cops did not find your body off the end of the Santa Monica pier, Reles is bunking at LAPD's Thai Town precinct. Sgt. Billy put a tracker on his pickup and the Samoan is watching the precinct's comings and goings from a restaurant across the street.

Reles must have a comfortable cot in there because Jeremy hasn't spotted him yet. Despite your best research and recon efforts, it's as if Hank Reles doesn't have a home. Whatever rock he lives under, he's good at keeping the address a secret. Once again, Reles proves better than you at your own game.

Finding him in a vulnerable place is up to Sgt. Billy's tracker and Jeremy. The restaurant owner doesn't mind if Jeremy keeps the table by the window as long as the big Samoan keeps eating. He complains he's eating so much he's going to develop a peanut allergy. You tell him to pay the restaurant owner more for the table rental and to pace himself eating his way through the menu.

Detective Mueller ran interference for Reles. He's not as good at keeping his home a secret. Sgt. Billy followed him home. Mueller can't hide because he's got a family and his wife spends her days taking the kids to school and to soccer. Then she documents their lives on Facebook. Detective Mueller wasn't hard to find. He's the soft target in the open, so Mueller will feel your wrath first.

When Sgt. Billy reports in, you give him his orders. He has a lot of stuff to shop for at Home Depot. A minute later, you call him back. "On second thought, Billy, go to several Home Depots. Load up. Don't attract attention. Make sure you aren't followed."

There's no getting at Reles, but if all goes well tonight, he'll be exactly where you need him to be.

At the appointed time, you spot Berb sprinting along the line of storage units. He's dressed for battle, just in case: yellow jumpsuit and all a la Bruce Lee in *Game of Death*. Uma Thurman looked great in the same outfit in *Kill Bill*. Chill gave Berb that outfit as a joke Christmas gift, but Berb loves it. He even started dieting and running more so he could fit into it.

You wish you were guarding Uma Thurman's body right about now. Or Legs. Life would be so much simpler if you could be the guy who sweeps Legs Gabrielle off her feet. Kevin Costner had his chance with Whitney Houston in *The Bodyguard*, but he walked away from her. That was the most unbelievable moment in a movie full of unbelievable moments. If all goes well with Mueller, you'll be able to walk away from this mess instead of being wheeled away.

Berbniak doesn't stop to chat and, judging by the amount of sweat he's pumping out, he's been running through the city for a while. A fast runner zig-zagging through back alleys is difficult for the FBI to follow surreptitiously. As he runs by, he doesn't even look your way. He drops the item you asked for. You wait a few minutes to see if the Feds show up. Just because Smith won't shoot you doesn't mean the rest of the FBI is so patient.

The Feds do not appear so you go out and retrieve the IronKey flash drive. Finally, it's statement making time. This one, everyone will remember.

RT STAY RIGHTEOUS.
@ASSASSINSPLAYBK

The smart ninja's friend is super glue. You've used it before to great effect. When Sgt. Billy returns, he confirms he's got everything on your shopping list. He's noted the make and model of the car Mueller drives, a 2014 Hyundai Sonata. Most important, that model has a sunroof and Mueller's house has a two-car garage.

The complication is the detective has a wife and two young girls who live with him. From the cell phone picture Sgt. Billy took, Mueller's wife is about thirty-five and blonde. The kids can't be more than five or six. Mueller's double life is going to be tough on them.

As night falls, you take off the Armani suit, slip into a black t-shirt, black jeans and black Nikes. Inspecting yourself in the shard of mirror taped to the steel wall, you look like any other hipster who should be shopping for a black beret on the way to a weeknight poetry slam at UCLA.

Clearly, something iconic is needed for the drama to come. A Scream Halloween mask might seem too funny.

A Billy puppet mask from the Saw movies would be appropriate. You looked into a Pinhead mask, but it cost too much. Instead, you top off your outfit with a *luchadore* mask. The Mexican wrestling mask is black with a skeleton's bone-white face and red flames around the eye slits. You hope the kids stay in bed and the wife is a deep sleeper.

It would be better if you stole a truck but Chill's van is already packed with your supplies. You look in the mirror again. Is this what a grown ass man should be doing?

Would Chill approve? *Thtay righteouth, Hey-thuth.*

You tell yourself you're doing this for Chill and for all the Gingers in the world. You probably should have given therapy more of a shot because you're also working through your own issues.

You reach under your shirt and trace the map of scars. The very first time Tia Marta cut you, she used the edge of an envelope. She laughed at you. You were so unused to pain then. Then she squeezed lemon juice into the paper cut. Soon she graduated to knives and salt. Then, the hot iron.

Looking back, you sure were a slow learner. But your whole life is a pile of shit, isn't it? Gotta start shoveling somewhere.

Tonight, ladies and gentlemen, the character of the clever hit man will be played by Jesus Diaz. The actor's motivation will be supplied by his lost childhood and tortured fool's soul.

Take a deep breath. Step closer to the mirror. Look into your eyes and try to find the man behind the scary mask. What happens tonight shouldn't be narrated by Morgan Freeman. Tough guy voice-over work for tonight's movie

173

should be supplied by the cowboy in the *Big Lebowksi*, Sam Elliot. Or maybe Dennis Leary could put a funny, edgy spin on what's about to unfold, like he does for those truck commercials.

Somebody really badass should play you. If John Leguizamo isn't available, could Jason Statham play a short Cuban?

RT SOLID @ASSASSINSPLAYBK
ADVICE: DON'T STEP IN THE BUTTER.

Magic tricks are fascinating. It's always disappointing to discover how they are achieved. For instance, when Detective Mueller pulls his Sonata into his garage and steps out of his car, you step out from behind his wife's car. Mueller is startled to see you come out of the shadows. All he sees is the bone white of the skull at first. What happens next only *looks* like magic.

By the time he processes that you're wearing a *luchadore* mask, he's focused on the muzzle of the pistol pointed at his head. The automatic garage door isn't quite down yet so he tries to make a run for it as he fumbles for his gun. Mueller is startled to see his feet in the air in front of him. He crashes to his back.

That's a cool magic trick.

The thin film of liquid butter on the floor converts the smooth soles of his dress shoes into surprise ice skates. See? Disappointing.

You land on his right arm first so he can't reach for the pistol in his shoulder harness under his left armpit. If he were a lefty, you might have had a problem, but since most people are right-handed, that's the way to bet. You go to work, pistol-whipping Mueller to soften him up. When he's tenderized, you reach for his weapon — a standard LAPD-issue revolver. Toss it aside.

It's late and the kids are in bed asleep. Mrs. Mueller is watching Jimmy Fallon in her bedroom on the second floor. You pause to listen for the pitter patter of little feet and complications. All you hear is Mueller's labored breathing. He's okay. It's labored because all your weight sits on his chest. One knee to the balls curls him up and in a moment you're rolling him face down.

When he tries to speak, you put the SIG's muzzle against his ear and whisper. "Sh. I've been in your house. Just on the first floor. If you make too much noise, I'll have to go read your kids a bedtime story. I found *Goodnight Moon* on the living room floor. Do you want me to read *Goodnight Moon* to your kids?"

He shakes his head.

"Good. Be quiet until I tell you to speak. I have questions. You will not speak until I'm ready. Otherwise it's *Goodnight Moon.*"

He's freaking out and bug-eyed but he stays quiet. You'd feel sorry for him, but you're bad and he's evil.

This is where Sam Elliot or Dennis Leary would say, *Try to remember that when you see what Jesus Diaz does next.*

When you look at Mueller, you don't see a cop who's a normal family man. You see a monster. You see a dead red-haired girl tied to a chair with half her head shaved. Her eyes stare, still wide and frightened, even into death. But now that you've kneed Mueller in the balls, Ginger's dead staring face sports a wide Joker grin.

176

This guy has daughters and he did that to somebody else's daughter? Unfathomable. Some things, no one should understand. Given the nature of Mueller's crimes, it's fitting you use a ball gag on him. Soaking the ball gag in vinegar and menthol is just an added touch to keep him distracted and his eyes watering while you manhandled him into position.

Use the extra-long zip ties to pin his wrists to each thigh, just above the knee. When he tries to get up, the buttered floor slams him back down into the concrete before you have a chance to do the same. Next, zip tie the ankles.

Next? This is complicated. Follow the checklist.

Don't step in the butter.

Make sure all the windows are rolled up (but leave a couple of inches down on the driver's side window.

Open the sunroof.

Pop the Sonata's hood.

Before you apply super glue to the car's steering wheel, it is critically important to disable the horn. In a moment, when Mueller discovers he can't take his hands off the wheel, he does the expected and slams his head into the center of the wheel. No car horn sounds because you ripped the wires. Now Mueller has a headache, though, so that was fun.

You cuff his ear with the SIG once, just because, and then blindfold him. You remove his tie and wrap it around his throat. Knot it behind the head rest to hold him still.

You've used piano wire and heavy fishing line in the past, but it's likely to cut your hands. Despite what every caper movie you've ever seen suggests, it's really hard to wear gloves and do delicate work like tying knots, especially when the adrenaline is pumping, your hands are shaking and time is a factor.

With the super glue applied to the wheel, you take out your carpet knife. The short, sharp, hooked blade fits precisely around any Adam's apple. It's also best for slipping under tight zip ties. Mueller resists putting his hand on the steering wheel, but he's got no leverage and a quick bash with your elbow into his solar plexus makes him cooperative. You take his handcuffs. They're good for smashing him in the face and opening up some deep cuts, too, but the fight is out of him so there's no need to be sadistic.

You want to be sadistic, but you don't need to be. That's the slim difference between you and your prey at this moment. You have prey. He has victims.

He doesn't give you a hard time placing his other hand on the steering wheel because, this time, after you cut the zip tie, you put the tip of the cold blade at his throat. Live and learn.

You pause to reflect on your work to make sure your tasks match your checklist. You made the mistake of putting super glue on a bad guy's palm once. Before you could glue him to the wall, he made a grab for your face and his hand came away furry. That was a painful lesson and you never could grow a beard again after that mishap.

You take off the *luchadore* mask. It's hot and sweaty. It's not half as hot and sweaty as Mueller is about to be.

Here's where Sam Elliot or Dennis Leary intone, *Don't try this at home, kids!*

RT HIT MEN: YOU'RE GOING TO NEED A COOL CODE NAME. @ASSASSINSPLAYBK

Double-check the door to the house. You've already cut the land line, super glued the back and front doors and you've taken the cell phone that was charging in the kitchen.

Creeping around the house barefoot and trying not to wake the kids or alert the wife was strangely more nerve wracking than beating up Mueller. You can't hit a kid or a woman. If one of the girls starts to cry, that would send you running. With the monster in the man suit, though? The easy answer is hit him harder.

You picked up the little rubber wedge for 99 cents from Dollarmania. It's still jammed safely under the door between the garage and the house so you won't be interrupted now. The most dangerous, and loudest part, is over. It's time for construction work to begin.

You bring out the cartons of foam insulation tubes. Each tube's application tip is already cut open and ready to go. It's the kind of insulation that expands to fill big

179

spaces behind walls as soon as it emerges from the tube. The instructions say it's good for "irregular spaces." Perfect. You begin with spraying the well at Mueller's feet. It comes out as a sticky beige cloud that quickly fills the space beneath the brake and accelerator.

He doesn't know what's going on and he's nervous. "Relax, Mr. Mueller. I won't set you on fire. I did that to Oswald and I hate to repeat myself. We don't want to suck the drama and tension from the moment, right?"

"Hmph?" he says through his gag.

It takes fewer tubes than you expected to get the car's cabin filled to his neck with foam insulation.

You slide the length of PVC pipe through the sunroof and line it up with his mouth. The super glue coats the edge of the circle of pipe. You remove the ball gag and jam the pipe over his mouth. You count to sixty to make sure it's secure. You repeat the procedure with a short length of pipe attached to his left ear.

You have extra tubes of insulation left over. You fill the rest of the Sonata's passenger compartment. It gives Mueller time to think and sweat. It gives the insulation time to harden.

By the time you're packed up and ready to whisper your questions down the tube and into his ear, Mueller is eager to answer. To be sure, you play tough guy a little harder.

"I already know the answers to several of my questions," you say. "You'll never know which ones so don't try to be cute. If I detect any deception on your part...I notice you like Coke, Mr. Mueller. You have a case in the corner of your garage. You're hot and itchy and terrified right now. Imagine how awful it will be when I start pouring Coke down that pipe until you drown. Now, if I say please, are you ready to answer my questions?"

His disembodied voice croaks up the PVC pipe. "Yes."

You have no doubt this is the most polite he's been to anyone. He gives you passwords. He tells you exactly what you need to know to bring down Detective Hank Reles. He knows nothing about Gaston Bekhti except he's from out East and he's rich. He doesn't know anything about the Spanish mob, either. He's never heard of Big Denny De Molina. That's okay. You have a feeling that, after tonight, the monsters will get flushed out of hiding.

Before you leave him to cook a while, you give him a small sip of Coke, but not enough to drown him. He'll live, if the cops come fast enough.

Your plan is not to call 911. That would lack imagination. Instead, you take the wedge out of the bottom of the door to the house and head for his computer. The files you need are in a deep sub-directory under old taxes labeled Gun Warranties. These files are not Gun Warranties. They are snuff films.

You don't have time to search through them all. Somewhere in there, video awaits of Ginger in the chair. Maybe Sugar's in the background in the cage screaming, "Don't!" You wish you hadn't come to the rescue too late.

You don't look at the videos. You don't want to watch Ginger die. Instead, you begin the email campaign.

You take out the IronKey flash drive and load the email addresses. Every network including the Fishing Channel gets a copy. Every journalist from CNN to the podcast networks gets a copy. Every address you have for the FBI and Homeland Security gets a copy. Everyone from Chill's list and from Detective Albrecht Mueller's address book gets the video files. That's just about everyone in the Los

Angeles Police Department.

Al's Mom will get the bad news, too.

The subject line reads: *Warning. Snuff films are in the attachments.*

You type a brief message:

Protect the identities of the victims. Stop these monsters: Gaston Bekhti, Detective Hank Reles and Detective Albrecht Mueller of the LAPD. This is what they do to women.
Detective Mueller is anxiously awaiting arrest in his home. He'll live, if you hurry. It's up to you if you decide to hurry.
Sincerely,
The Divine Assassin

You really like the sound of "The Divine Assassin." If you get out of this clean, that's what you'll call yourself all the time. Sure, it'll sound obnoxious after a while, but when it comes down to it, we are all defined by what we do.

The moment you click send is perfect except that *The Tonight Show* is long over. Mueller's wife stands in the doorway with a shiny .38 pointed at your head.

If she doesn't shoot you to death, you promise yourself you'll flee to Canada. In Canada, not every goddamn house is an arsenal.

RT HAVE SOME STYLE. DON'T BE JOE GUNSLINGER. @ASSASSINSPLAYBK

She stands in the doorway, taking you in. You're wearing the *luchadore* mask again. It's a good bet she didn't see that coming when she pulled on her jeans this morning. You aren't terribly worried, though her hand is shaking and that's the hand that's holding the gun.

"Good evening, Mrs. Mueller. May I call you Marsha?"

Her eyes widen. "How do you know my name?"

"*Sh*. The girls are sleeping and we don't want to disturb them."

"I'm calling the police."

"I already did, after a fashion. They'll be here soon."

"Good, then. We'll wait."

You decide to like her then. She's scared out of her mind but she's standing her ground. It would have been smarter to hide in her kids' room and cower, pointing her gun at the door. Still, Marsha Mueller is spunky.

"Did you call on your cell phone, mister? The phone doesn't work. If you lie to me, I'll shoot you right here."

The threat sounds so close to what you told her

husband, you have to nod your appreciation. It's a good threat and you have no intention of lying to this woman. You take off the mask and give her a small smile. "Marsha? Why don't you hold that pistol in both hands and relax your elbows a bit. You're so stiff and nervous, you're shaking. If you could point it a little off target, just enough to avoid an unhappy accident, that would be great. Please."

"I'll shoot you if you try anything!"

"I don't doubt it. I'm not going to move from this chair. I just need to show you something and then we can talk some more or wait for the cops. Whatever you want to do, okay? You've got the gun. I'm sitting down. You can see my hands. You're in control, okay? Can I show you something now?"

You don't wait for her answer. Instead, you spin the laptop around and press enter. Her ice-blue eyes widen so much you see the whites all the way around her irises.

"This isn't the decoy laptop you use for Facebook and Pinterest, Marsha. I found this one in the back of the closet, just where Al said I'd find it, hidden between two boxes of old LPs in a shopping bag. That's your husband doing that, Marsha."

Her lip curls. Her lips tremble. She wants to look away and she can't.

"That's an innocent girl he's doing that to. There's nothing consensual happening there, is there? Al and Hank are having fun. See their smug smiles, so secure in the knowledge they will never be caught? You probably know Hank, I'm guessing. Does he come over on the fourth of July? Join the barbeque, maybe? Does he play with your kids? I've come to stop Hank and your husband

184

from doing these — "

The gun drops to the floor with a heavy *thunk*. She throws up.

"...atrocities."

This is the first time you've disarmed anyone by making them vomit.

You pull her up from her knees and rub her back. "Easy. You'll be okay. He's not hurting anyone anymore. I saw to that."

She heaves again and coughs and sputters. The floor of the Mueller family's den tells you she had Kung Pao chicken for dinner.

When Marsha's finished, she straightens and wipes drool from her chin. "Is Al dead?"

You look at your watch. "No. Not yet, barring unforeseen circumstances."

"Where is he?"

"In the car. In the garage."

Marsha Mueller scoops up the pistol and races out of the room. You grab the IronKey drive from the laptop's USB port and your mask from the desk. You leave to follow her. Then you double back and close the laptop in case the kids get up.

When you enter the garage, Marsha is yelling at Al. Judging by the weak voice of hot misery creeping out of the black PVC pipe sticking out of the Sonata's sunroof, Al Mueller is still alive and probably wishing he wasn't.

"Gee-zuzz! Why didn't you just kill him?" Marsha asks.

You blink. You're not sure. The quick and easy answer is, Chill's wishes were that you be more imaginative. He always thought you could be better than the average Joe Gunslinger. Or maybe you worried that if you tortured and shot Mueller, you'd like it too much and you'd become him. You got what you needed and no more.

Oddly, you don't regret letting him live. That's new. A cop in a deviant sex ring who is also murderer of young women? Prison will be hard. Death would let him off too easy.

Marsha's staring at you, still waiting for an answer. Why did you let him live?

You clear your throat. "Um. Because…reasons."

Thtay righteouth, Hey-thuth.

RT LEARN THE BASKET HOLD. @ASSASSINSPLAYBK

She raises the gun, pointing it at the Sonata's windshield. You sweep one arm up under her arm. One shot is fired into the ceiling and now she's fighting you. Marsha Mueller tries to push you back, punches your chest and slaps your face. You step behind her as you twist the gun from her hand. You toss the gun behind you and grab her wrists in a basket hold, pinning her crossed arms.

"Sh. Marsha. You've got kids. I've seen their pictures. They're still little. You pull that trigger and you won't see them except at Thanksgiving and Christmas and your birthday. Read me?"

"Did he? Did he touch my girls?" She's weeping.

"I don't know, Marsha. But whatever happened or didn't, they'll get help. You'll get help. It's going to be okay, but you've got to do as I tell you now. Don't kill him. Your daughters are going to need you."

The fight drains from her. Her knees are weak. You let her slide to the floor. Mueller is trying to scream.

The cops will be here soon. "Marsha, do you know a

man named Gaston? Gaston Bekhti?"

She stares at the car blankly and shakes her head.

"Are you sure? It's important. He's described to me as an older man, silver hair. Maybe an old guy you know by another name with an accent?"

"No."

She's staring at the car and listening to her husband beg to be let out of the oven created by his body heat. She's staring at the checklist you slapped on the hood. You left it as a present for the FBI.

At the bottom of the checklist you used to spring Detective Mueller's trap, you added a note. It reads:

Special thanks to Agent John Smith of the FBI for making this possible. Also, kudos to Big Denny De Molina for paying John not to arrest me.

You wanted to be a hero, John. You put off murdering me and I appreciate it. Now you are a hero.

You're welcome,
The Divine Assassin

You stiffen when you hear a tiny voice behind you, coming from the kitchen. Marsha is deep in shock and she doesn't hear it. You slip back into the house.

A little blonde girl, about five, looks up at you, bewildered and trying to rub sleep out of her eyes. Kids shouldn't be awakened by gunshots. Kids should have a childhood. You didn't, but maybe the girl and her sister will have a chance at one now.

"Where's Mommy?"

"She's with Daddy. They're having a grown-up talk."

"Who are you?"

"Right now?" You smile wide. "Right now I'm the babysitter."

"*Not* a baby."

You crouch. "You're right. You aren't a baby. Or you're very tall for a baby. I don't know about that. Maybe you're the world's tallest baby."

She smiles.

"It's way past your bedtime, isn't it? What's your name?"

"Cindy."

"Cindy. Of course! You're Cindy Lou Who. And you're out of bed. You better go back to bed, okay?"

The kid doesn't move.

"Go back to bed…please."

She holds out her hand. "You're the babysitter? Really?"

"Yep. Professionally."

"We never had a *boy* babysitter."

"Well. That doesn't seem fair, does it?"

"I want a bedtime story."

"I bet you and your sister already had a bedtime story tonight."

"Want another one," she whines.

Her hand is so small and delicate in your palm.

When the first uniforms arrive, they'll find Marsha in the garage standing next to the car. The Sonata will be filled with beige clouds of quick-set foam insulation and muted screams.

You've made a statement. You've announced to the world you aren't a terrorist. You're no Iron Man or Thor, but you're an avenger.

Maybe you aren't so far gone that you can at least aspire to a Robert Downey Jr.-level of awesome.

RT FIREFIGHTERS DON'T LIKE BEING CALLED BUCKETHEADS & BASEMENT SAVERS. #COPTALK

You imagine Marsha telling Al Mueller how much she hates him through the PVC tube glued to his ear, dripping well-deserved hate into his fetid brain. The first uniforms on the scene will call the fire department to cut Mueller out. The cops will find both girls asleep in their beds, tucked in tight and safe.

The LAPD claims a response time of 5.7 minutes. Despite your massive email campaign, they take ten minutes to get to Al's house. According to your scanner, they waited for a supervisor so they take fifteen minutes to set up a perimeter to secure the scene.

You keep one eye on the clock as you drive away in Chill's surveillance van. You listen to the chatter on the police scanner as red, white and blue strobes flash by. You have to grin about the hyper-response. The scene is just so weird, are they really calling for backup? Or are they calling their buddies to have a look before the bucketheads and basement savers cut Mueller out with the jaws of life?

They don't need backup now. They need an ambulance, Child Protective Services and CSI. The Golden State's teams that deal with trouble will pick up the pieces and put the puzzle together. Somebody will help those kids. The girls have a chance at a life now, but you had to break the lie they had first.

Marsha Mueller will change her name and she'll never really trust anyone again. She won't want to talk about the betrayal and how deeply she was deceived. She'll blame herself. Someone will tell her she should forgive him. Someone well-meaning will say poor Al was mentally ill. Marsha will hate those people almost as much as she hates her soon-to-be ex. Her rage will always be close at hand, ready to fire.

At least, that's how you handled it.

But sometimes, in moments like these, you can pause to relax. After all that relentless action, you take just a moment for a deep breath to reflect on an elaborate job well done. The escape was the smoothest part of the mission.

It took you a couple of minutes to slip out of a second-floor window and drop to the ground. Jumping the neighbor's fence took a few more seconds.

You didn't get away by much. Little Cindy drove a hard bargain. To avoid waking her sister sleeping in the next bed, you read her a bedtime story. She insisted you read it twice. Fortunately, *Goodnight Moon* is a short book.

You enjoyed reading to the girl more than you enjoyed stewing her father in a car made into a crock pot. Chill would have been proud of you.

Maybe you *aren't* still you. Not quite.

You allow yourself to feel good about that for another

whole minute. You feel…what is that unfamiliar feeling? *Pure.* You feel pure.

The Divine Assassin bit started as a cutesy joke. However, heading to Legs Gabrielle's house to debrief and smoke a joint with Sgt. Billy, you feel high in a way that feels like falling in love.

No.

You feel like you *deserve* somebody's love and not just anybody's love. Maybe Legs will swoon at your exploits. You could spin what started as a wicked torture story into a clever caper. Maybe you will escape to Canada. Maybe Legs can shoot more movies in Vancouver or Toronto. Maybe this is the start of a beautiful friendship (with benefits).

Chill's voice pops into your head with a cheery, *Groovy, baby! I can dig it!*

Your smile fades when the scanner chatter heats up from Thai Town. While you were congratulating yourself, Detective Hank Reles shot and killed two uniformed cops as they tried to arrest him.

Shut your mouth.

It's not over.

RT @ASSASSINSPLAYBK 47,000 PEOPLE ON THE NO-FLY LIST. SOON? JUST A FLY LIST.

You won't be slipping away and across the Canadian border anytime soon. Like you, Reles is now a desperate fugitive. You're pretty sure he won't flee to Canada, either. Not yet.

Last you checked, the powers that be had 47,000 people on the No-fly list. Of the 680,000 stuck on the KST list — "known or suspected terrorists" — almost half have no known affiliation with a terrorist group. That's many more than the number of those on the watch list for Al Qaeda, Hamas and Hezbollah combined. The government keeps adding to the pile at a rate of 900 new names a day. No wonder they can't keep track of you.

Reles knows what you know. The powers that be won't catch him, either. They're too busy adding to the pile of names they can't manage. Maybe they'll realize their mistake when everybody's on the watch list.

Domestically, the spy agencies concentrate their watch list efforts on New York. Since 9/11, that makes sense. But the city they watch most, after New York, is Dearborn, Michigan. With only 96,000 people, it has a high percentage of Arab-American names in the phone book. The counterterrorism agencies keep staring at groups as perpetual suspects instead of focusing on deserving individuals. Despite all their tech, the alphabet agencies have buried themselves in data so deep, you have to wonder if they're out to stop real terror threats. Or is Homeland Security just another employment program for the otherwise unemployable, like massive infantry hires in the time of drones?

China builds one out of every four cars in the world. Japan is second. Germany comes in third, then South Korea and India. Finally, your beloved USA comes in sixth. America used to build cars. Now they manufacture law enforcement, prison guard jobs and paranoia.

You heard these factoids on NPR because sometimes you joined Chill on protection details. Chill was always good company and a good conversationalist (as long as you shut up while he listened to *Wait, Wait, Don't Tell Me*).

You wish you'd spent more time sitting in cars with Chill and just talking. He had the body and presence to be an intimidating bodyguard, but it seemed he got into the business because he really loved celebrity gossip. You wish Chill was here now.

Big Brother's ability to peer through every web cam, ATM camera, and stoplight cam won't help. They can sift through every bank record and credit card transaction, but the feds still couldn't stop a couple of kids from bombing the Boston Marathon. How are they going to stop a cop if the cop is smart?

From what you've seen, Reles is smart and Sugar says

Bekhti has money. They've got the resources to escape. If they hole up until the heat dies down, they could be at large and destroying lives for a long time to come. Theoretically, Reles and Bekhti could be on a boat and in the wind already.

But no, Reles is not going anywhere yet. He'll want to end his time in Los Angeles on a win. When you push a monster, no matter how smart they are, they push back. That's what monsters do. He's going to want the human prize with whom he has been so obsessed. He'll want to make a statement.

You call Sgt. Billy.

"Hey, Chief."

"On my way. Circle the wagons."

"They're already circled, Ace. Legs and Sugar are locked up tight and I'm on the castle wall ready with burning oil in case there's a siege."

"Double the guard on the Princess's chamber. Everyone in to protect the castle?"

"Skunk and Berb are here with me, armed and ready."

"What about the kid?"

That's how you find out Jeremy the Samoan isn't answering his phone.

You call and call again. When Jeremy doesn't pick up, cold spider feet run down your spine and hot sweat trickles down your face. He was supposed to be watching for Reles. Reles must have been watching for the Samoan.

You tell yourself the battery on Jeremy's cell could be dead. You try to come up with more scenaria where Jeremy doesn't try to play the hero against a cop who has just killed two cops. You worry that you and the crew ribbed the newbie too much and now maybe Jeremy's done something stupid to try to prove himself. Or maybe the kid is a goof who is stuck on the toilet because he's stuffed himself with too much pad thai.

But in your heart you already know. America manufactures paranoia now, but in your experience, paranoia is rarely wrong.

Your cell lights, vibrates and plays the chorus to ZZ Top's *Sharp Dressed Man.*

It's Jeremy's cell number showing in the caller ID.

Of course, it's not Jeremy.

RT MILLION DOLLAR PHONE APP IDEA
@ASSASSINSPLAYBK #WWJD?

"Hello, Jesus."

You expected Reles to call you Armando. This is bad. How does he know your name? "Let me talk to Jeremy. I need proof of life."

"No can do."

"Then we don't have anything to talk about."

You hang up. Too bad you can't hang up on anyone dramatically anymore. That used to be a thing you could do with a phone, hang up with a clatter and a bang and a loud, indignant click. Somebody should write an app to replicate the experience.

The cell lights up again.

You answer, "Sex line. Ramone the Sexy Vampire speaking."

"Jesus! If you hang up on me ag — "

You hang up.

Reles must be seething. A monster like him, treating people the way he does, is all about control. Deny him anything and his rage is dangerous. You might have just sealed the Samoan's fate. Or he was dead already. It's so easy to make a tactical error when you're pressed for time and dealing with lunatics. You prefer the organization a checklist provides.

Maybe Alaska is your answer. Anywhere the population is spread thin is the place for you. More people close together? More friction. Friction means heat and heat leads to burns. Unfortunately, you don't imagine there are many hermits with a penchant for Armani suits and Tanino Crisci shoes. It's hard to get a good latte, go to the movies and enjoy a quiet afternoon in a bookstore when you're hiding out from humanity high above the Arctic Circle.

You drive. You sweat. You count slowly to one hundred. You tell yourself you'll call back when you reach one hundred, but you force yourself to take a deep breath with each number. You're afraid the next time you answer the phone it will be Jeremy screaming. Instead, it's Jeremy.

"He's got a gun to my head, Jesus."

"Hang in there, kid." (That's about the stupidest thing a man has ever said to anyone, but what else is there?)

Reles comes back on the line. "Proof of life."

"Good for you. You've just bought yourself one of your testicles back."

"What?"

"You've let Jeremy live. I'm going to let you keep a testicle for that demonstration of good judgment."

"You don't seem to understand. I've got your little buddy hostage."

"Barely know him. Don't care. What do you want?"

"I need you to pick up some stuff for me. Do that and your Gilligan lives."

"My Gilligan? Haven't heard that one in a long time."

"I like old television. I used to watch a lot of old TV."

"Me, too. I prefer old movies…and candlelight dinners and long walks on the beach. What do you want me to pick up at your house?"

"You're swift."

"If you could do it yourself, you would. Thanks to a bunch of videos just released everywhere, you can't leave whatever rock you're hiding under, can you? What's the matter? Gaston wouldn't do it for you?"

"Gaston isn't answering my calls. Guess he ran away."

He gives you the address. You plug it into the van's GPS. Then he tells you what he wants. There's a go-bag in the back of his bedroom closet.

"There will probably be cops there already, Reles."

"That's your problem."

"Okay."

"Call me back in two hours and I'll tell you where to drop the go-bag. I get the bag, you get your Gilligan."

"I'll call you back in two hours and we'll meet at my place. Top floor of the building — "

"Your dump over Big In Japan?"

"Er…yeah." He's showing off, telling you he's still way ahead of you and even had time to map the territory.

"Yeah, well, we'll just have to negotiate about negotiating after you've got my bag," he says. There's laughter behind his tone. "Back of the upstairs closet. Get it. Get it?"

"Peachy. Anything else?"

"Just one thing. They're plastering my name and picture over every channel!"

"Gee, I wonder why?"

"My picture's on TMZ right now! It's behind George Clooney!"

"Yeah?"

"How did you get George Clooney's email address?"

"The man whose skull you fractured? Chill Gillie? He had a lot of cool friends and they all want you dead."

"Okay...but George fucking *Clooney*? He's holding a press conference about me? My name is trending as a hashtag on Twitter! That and #YesAllWomen. It's crazy."

"Congrats, Reles. You're a celebrity. I've been meaning to get on Twitter myself, actually. Catch the news, follow some of the people I've been watching out for...maybe tweet some inspirational quotes or something."

"Sure, that's nice for you. George Clooney is mad at me! Tell me, what's he really like?"

"Maybe he'll do lunch with you if you turn yourself in, Reles. How bad do you want to get to know the real George?"

You hang up and try to figure out how you can get the go-bag and save Jeremy. He only gave you two hours so there's no time for stealth. The crime scene in Mueller's house is fresh so you're hoping the LAPD isn't too organized yet. However, it's probably too much to hope that the city's police force will have a slower response time than TMZ and Clooney's publicist.

If there are only a few uniforms in the house, you'll have to try a hit and run. How are you going to do that without hurting somebody who is just doing their job? You feel good and pure, but it's going to be difficult maintaining your good-guy mojo as The Divine Assassin. As you speed on to your destination in Pacific Heights, it seems kind of fitting that the word *assassin* has two asses in it.

You tell yourself you'll improvise once you get there, but going in? You have no idea how to execute the mission without trading shots and maybe executing a few cops.

What would Jesus do?

RT DON'T BE A HIT MAN, UNLESS THE HIT IS MUSIC & YOU'RE JAY-Z. @ASSASSINSPLAYBK

If Jeremy knew the closest you can park to the address Reles gave you is two blocks, he'd pray harder. The street is blocked with fire engines. There's no fire, but they're ready for one.

You'd hoped the cops would still be reeling and acting dumb. Instead, with two cops dead by Reles's hand, they're working faster, sticking to that 5.7 minute average response time. LAPD has swooped in with all their forces. Judging by their numbers, the police are well aware of Reles's military background and they're worried about IEDs. You don't see one way to complete your mission to get the bag and save the Samoan.

The crowd stares down the street with a mixture of anxiety and anticipation. People say they go to the Indianapolis 500 race to watch cars turn left at high speeds. Everyone knows the real entertainment is in watching beer cans rattle from the deafening noise and wondering when somebody's going to die ugly. Pacific

Heights feels like the Indy 500 tonight.

You ask the nearest guy in a bathrobe what's going on. He tells you to shut up and get yourself a TV. Then he turns back to staring down the street. You want to smack him, but his casual rudeness also makes you homesick for New York. You let it pass.

An elderly woman touches your elbow. "I'm Eleanor," she says. She smiles and gives you a flirty wink. "Don't mind him. He's grouchy. The police told us to evacuate. There's a fugitive in the neighborhood."

The nearest fugitive is you. You return the woman's smile.

She looks in your eyes and touches her hair. She straightens to push out her chest. She's pretty old, but the breast implants are probably no more than half her age. Breast implants have been around since the sixties. You suspect Eleanor was one of the brave, early pioneers. Her thick collagen lips are new, too.

You don't know for sure what's going on in her head. However, you're pleased to get a few seconds' relaxation from being on a suicide mission for a maniac. You sigh. It's flattering that you can still inspire an eighty-year-old to flirt.

The numerous beatings and breaks you've received over time have made your nose a little thicker and angle a little to the right. You used to be pretty. Now you've got what Big Denny called, "tough-guy good looks." That means you've got a bad case of thug mug. Your features are coarsening. At least you never got cauliflower ears.

If you thought your chances of living another night were better, you'd worry about the trend your face is following. You're suddenly past thirty and there is no little house with a picket fence, or a wife and a couple of kids in your future. You should have been a lawyer. When divorce attorney's think like merciless assassins, they make long paper.

You thought you'd improvise, but you still have no ideas. The big Samoan is still screwed to the wall. There's just no way to ninja your way in. Too many cops and too many bright lights. Reles's house doesn't just have a few policemen surrounding it. The bomb squad is here. Once they give the all clear, a small crowd of investigators will crawl through the house in booties, masks and white overalls.

If there were fewer cops to blow past — and if you had a fake badge — you might have considered bluffing your way in. You'd still have a hard time walking out of the scene with a bag over your shoulder. Everything has to be bagged and tagged. If Hank Reles still has a teddy bear from childhood in there, it's considered evidence.

If you had a few days, you might have been able to set up diversions all over town, use some magic misdirection and maybe set up a few harmless explosions on office tower rooftops. There's no way you can get in and out.

"They sure moved fast to block off the street, huh?" you say.

The old man in the bathrobe looks your way again. "That's my next-door neighbor's house. Hank Reles. Borrows my lawn mower twice a month and hasn't refilled the damn gas tank once."

"Well...you should have guessed he was criminally insane, then, huh?"

RT BLACK BAG OPS ARE ALWAYS MORE DANGEROUS THAN YOU THINK. @ASSASSINSPLAYBK

"This is my husband, Uri," the old woman says.

"Pleased to meet you both." You shake her hand. "I'm J.D."

Uri ignores you and stands on his tiptoes to try to get a better look through the crowd. He doesn't notice when she holds your hand and won't let go.

"Do you think they'll let us get back to our bed soon, J.D.? I really need to get back to my nice warm bed right now. Don't you?"

"Um…dunno."

"How long do you think this will take?" she asks.

You shrug. "Did the police give you any hint?"

"They said they'd give us an estimate when they knew. That was twenty minutes ago."

"I saw a bomb squad truck," Uri says. "Hank's Special Forces or something. I thought that was hooey, but I guess they're taking him seriously."

"They have to, dear," Eleanor says. "It's all over the

news. Horrible sex crimes that man was involved in. Murder is so unnecessary."

The old lady looks at you in a way you recognize and you shift your weight from foot to foot uncomfortably.

"Hank is a good-looking young man," she says. "It's terrible, treating women like that. Doesn't he know there's plenty of opportunities on the Internet? Latex and leather and whips and chains and whatnot? Just about everything a body needs." She looks you up and down and licks her lips slowly. "It can be so good. It doesn't have to be mean. Do you know what I mean, J.D.? I bet you do."

When you tear your gaze off Eleanor, Uri's staring at you and his wife. "This isn't the time, Eleanor! For God's sake, girls are dead, woman!"

She straightens and seems like a prim grandmother for a moment. "Yes, Uri. I know. It's sick. It's a terrible thing to do to a person, especially to young girls. It's such a waste! When will pigs like Hank understand that no means no? All this sex and violence comes out of repression, I think. The most conservative places in the world always download the freakiest porn, don't you know?"

You realize she's still holding your hand when she gives a little squeeze with bony, Crypt Keeper fingers and adds, "No means no and yes means yes."

"Um." You pull your hand away gently.

She leans closer. "Uri's right. Now is not the time. But..." Eleanor whispers, "when it is the time, Uri and I swing."

"Eleanor! Have you got an off button?"

"Shut up, you old bastard! You couldn't find *my* on button with a map and a gynecologist to guide you!"

People turn to stare and giggle. You take a step to the left, slowly melting back from the crowd. This, you suspect, is the quintessential Hollywood moment. Old people who were young when they came west lived life a little crazy and never really backed away from the edge. But maybe old people have sex lives in Utah, too.

You check your watch. Ten minutes before time's up.

The answer comes to you. Call Reles and tell him you have the go-bag. He said it was a black bag. Jeremy's only chance is for you to go buy one on the way to the rendezvous. You have to take the chance the bags will look alike, at least long enough for you to put a bullet in the monster's head. It's dark. Maybe you can sell it.

Uri and Eleanor yell louder and you step back, out of the press of bodies. Everyone is watching the elderly couple yell angrily at each other.

Everyone but John Smith of the FBI, of course. The one agent who can most easily pick you out of a crowd does so. You turn to find his pistol pointed at your nose.

"Hi," you say.

"Hi."

Two beefy guys clamp their hands on you and force you to the ground. All three yell at you to comply or they'll shoot you in the head. One screamer slinging one set of orders would have been sufficient.

Smith takes your SIG, the knife in your sock and your phone. Strong hands cuff your wrists behind your back. When they pull you up, Smith smiles wide. "Jesus Salvador Umberto Luis Diaz AKA Dr. J.D. Fix! You are under arrest for multiple counts of murder and domestic terrorism. Who are the fossils you were talking to?"

"Reles's neighbors. Don't really know them. They

208

seem...nice."

Smith glances at one of his fellow agents and tells him to question the old couple. "Be sure to get their names and addresses. I'll send them a fruit basket. If not for them, I would never have spotted Mr. Diaz in the crowd. Anything to say now, smart ass?"

"Shit."

RT NO HIT MAN BELIEVES IN FREE WILL. IT'S ALWAYS EXPENSIVE. @ASSASSINSPLAYBK

Smith gets excited when you tell him about the go-bag. He seems less concerned about rescuing Jeremy. He's sure whatever's in the bag must be valuable evidence. He marches you past the yellow crime scene tape and up the block to Reles's house.

It's just another two-story house indistinguishable from all the others. You aren't sure what you expected. It's not like the mailbox is made of human skulls. It's just another house where, until very recently, a monster lived. How many other houses hold monsters? Or maybe you're still a little freaked out by Eleanor and Uri. Is anybody really normal or is that just one of those things everyone pretends to believe? Maybe normal is like Bigfoot. Everybody says it's out there somewhere but proof is thin on the ground.

Agent Smith gets into a huddle with his team out of your earshot. You can't hear the words but you recognize the tone. Urgent orders are being slung and men with guns are running somewhere, bent on a task that could get them killed.

"I didn't much like that note you left at Mueller's house," Smith says. "However, given who you are and who I am, you're not doing me any damage."

"Nobody listens to Jesus."

"Goddamn right." Smith sits you in the back of a cruiser in the street in front of the house. They bag your weapons and put them in the trunk. You're beside the bomb squad truck but if you lean, you can see the house well enough.

Smith keeps the cruiser's back door open and sweeps his arm toward the house in a magnanimous gesture. "After what you did for us with Detective Mueller," he says, "you deserve a front row seat to the show. That was a hell of a thing. I've never seen anyone work that hard to fuck somebody up."

"I've lived through worse for much longer. Does all this newfound gratitude mean you aren't going to shoot me?"

He chuckles. "Oh, I have a strong feeling I'm still going to shoot you. But every Christmas Eve, I'll toast you with some eggnog and, for a second or two? I'll have a doubt about whether I made the right decision."

"Sounds reasonable." You try to look cool, but you don't really know if he's just busting balls or not. Back in New York, you did imply you were willing to kill his family to get what you wanted. Technically. Smith seems the type to hold a grudge.

The FBI agent directs the bomb squad tech searching the house to the upstairs bedroom to search the closet.

"Did you check the basement first?"

Smith looks annoyed but nods. "Yeah. We thought we'd

find bones or a dozen bodies chained to the walls. Instead, I'm told Reles has a really kickass man cave. Sectional couch with a beer fridge and a huge HD TV. My bet was there'd be at least a couple of girls from the Dominican or Guatemala down there. Those are the hot countries for human trafficking right now."

"His video collection will be hideous," you say.

"Yeah, we know our jobs, Jesus."

"Sure."

"You used to be an MP, huh?"

"You've read my file a hundred times, I'm sure."

"What makes a guy like you, anyway?"

"Violent video games and too much corn syrup in the after school snacks?"

He cuffs your ear. It hurts but you try not to let that show. "Sorry. I didn't think it was a serious question. I didn't realize you were trying to have a moment with me."

Smith cuffs you again in the same spot. Your eyes bug and your left ear rings.

"So," Smith asks, "what makes a guy like you, anyway?"

"Lack of choices."

"Everybody's got a choice."

"Then why aren't you a hit man, Agent Smith?"

"Because that's a stupid choice."

"When did you decide that?"

Smith smiles. "You're asking me if I sat down with my high school guidance counselor and went over my options? Law enforcement or killing people for money?"

"So, no. You didn't make the choice, one way or the other. How do you know you really had any choice at all, then? You say you know your job. Okay. Maybe you became what you are because that's what you're good at. That's your design. That's not a choice. You were a calf in high school who thinks he made a choice to be a cow for the rest of his life."

The FBI Agent looks at you for a moment before telling you to shut the fuck up.

"I don't just kill for money, by the way. Sometimes it's just called being righteous."

Smith hits you again, harder. You decide this is an excellent time to choose to shut up. Free will and all that.

RT WITH BOMBS, ALWAYS ASSUME THERE'S MORE THAN ONE DEVICE. @ASSASSINSPLAYBK

Smith asks an LAPD lieutenant if the bomb tech has found the bag in the upstairs closet yet.

"We don't want to rush it, sir. LAPD says we take it slow to ensure there are no booby traps."

"This guy wasn't about those kinds of boobies. He's a pathetic perve, pure and simple."

You aren't usually the type to blurt things, but to everything there is a season. "No! Take it slow! He was Spec Ops before he was LAPD!"

Agent Smith whirls on you. "But he was *always* a perve. Kind of like you, huh? A torturer, right? You and Reles share lots in common, I bet." He punches you in the gut and you fold up.

When you can get your breath, you say through clenched teeth, "Owie! That's a nasty menstrual cramp I've got going on."

A couple of cops standing nearby burst out laughing. They turn their attention back to Reles's house when

Smith gives them a dirty look.

The radio chatter goes back and forth. The bomb tech has found an impressive weapons cache. With these guys, there's always a huge weapons cache, isn't there?

You wonder what Cuba will be like. It's been a long time since you were in Cuba, but you were on the other side of the island. Guantanamo Bay won't be quite as nice. There's a bunch of innocent guys there who will never get out. There's a few real assholes who will also never get out. They'll ask you to commit to their hunger strike but the tubes they use for force feeding are an absolute misery. You don't have the stomach for it. Once again, you don't have that many choices in life. Suicide by cop is still an option.

Then you have a chilling thought. The government has Rendition and Detention sites all over the world. What if they send you to a secret prison in the Middle East? The food there would (almost) make you wish you were detained in Gitmo.

On the other hand, Agent Smith has promised to shoot you. He probably hasn't forgotten that.

The bomb squad's radio receiver in the nearby truck is turned up. "I found a bag in the upstairs closet. It's a black bag."

"Smith! Let me call Reles."

"We've already got the number off your phone, dumbass. We don't need you to call him. SWAT's already got a team coming down on him as we speak. They're zeroing in. We don't need you to do our jobs."

"Let me call Reles, anyway. I'll tell him I've got what he wants. At least if he thinks I'm coming with his stuff, maybe he won't do damage to his hostage. I can talk to him, distract him while your guys get into position."

"They're almost there, Diaz. I don't need you talking to Reles and spooking him. If there is a hostage, we have pros to deal with that. You're a murdering, torturing scumbag. You are in my custody. You will not be in contact with our target. Understand?"

"The guy he's got. He's just a kid, Smith. He's been a bodyguard for a few weeks."

"I'm not responsible for his poor vocational choices. Or maybe your theory is right and he was *designed* to be a sacrificial cow."

"Smith, you must have been designed to be a prick."

The bomb squad's radio clicks on again. "It's a device."

The cops and firefighters go quiet.

Shit. Reles didn't want anything except to blow you up. That seems oddly personal for a guy you met only once. Most bad guys meet you a few times before they feel that strong an urge to burn you in hell.

Smith turns to you with the kind of toothy grin that makes you want to knock each tooth down his throat one by one with a small piano-tuning hammer.

"No problem," the bomb tech says. "It's crude. And… disarmed."

Everybody relaxes and Smith's laughing at you as his cell rings. The FBI agent who's liaising with LAPD SWAT reports they've found Reles' hideout. It's a warehouse in West Hollywood.

Smith puts the caller on speaker and stares into your eyes as the happy report comes in.

"They have eyes on the hostage. Alive."

Jeremy is alive!

"Looks like he's alone, tied to a chair."

216

Wait. The phone is there, but Reles isn't?

Time for more blurting. "No!" you shout. "*T-t-trap!* Reles is — "

The explosion in West Hollywood cuts off your warning and finishes your argument for you.

It takes a moment before the FBI agent comes back on the line. "Smith! We've got men down! The whole *building* came down!"

Sorry, Jeremy.

Smith curses. The radio cross-chatter sounds like a fight. Amid all the angry and urgent conversations, only you seem to hear the bomb tech in Reles's house. Over the open channel, he says, "Uh-oh."

You lie down on the cruiser's back seat and then roll to the floor.

Take a breath. Screw eyes tight.

RT HOW TO STINK UP THE PLACE
@ASSASSINSPLAYBK

The explosion doesn't bring down Reles's entire house, but the concussive wave feels like a padded hammer in the chest.

You bring your knees up and pull the handcuffs under your heels. It's a tight squeeze but if Javier Bardem can do it in *No Country for Old Men*, a ninja like you should be able to do it. It looked easier in the movie but you manage to get your hands in front of you without dislocating a shoulder.

When you pop your head up for a quick peek, people in the street are picking themselves up off the ground. You crane your neck but you don't see much smoke or dust. This moment of confusion would have been a good time to run, but Agent Smith is at the door with his gun out and pointed at your chest shaking his head. He looks judgmental and jittery.

A bomb specialist in full gear stumbles out of the front door and a cloud of thin, white smoke pours out after him. He's waving his arms wildly. Everyone stops and stares for a couple of seconds, more than a little amazed as the tech falls off the front steps. A group of cops and firefighters rush forward to help the man, but several slow and then drop back.

A senior firefighter waves the group back. The cops stumble toward the street, coughing and heaving. Two firefighters pull their oxygen masks up from their Scott Air Packs and rush forward. They grip the bomb tech under his armpits to yank him away from the advancing cloud. With his heavy gear, it's a hard slog but they pull him across the grass. The senior firefighter is screaming, but his mask makes him incomprehensible until he's halfway to the street.

"Carbide! *Carbide bomb! Carbide gas!*"

Calcium carbide, when exposed to air or water, makes a big boom. It also produces a cloud of noxious gas. Reles must have used a lot of carbide for the secondary device. A little carbide can kill gophers. A lot sends humans screaming and gasping.

Everyone's forced back to the street, but it seems the carbide bomb hasn't killed anyone. If Reles wanted mass casualties…this doesn't make much sense. What purpose would a carbide bomb serve?

Agent Smith notices your hands are no longer behind your back and he leans into the car. He smacks the back of your head and pushes you down to the floor by the back of your neck. "I won't have to shoot you, Jesus. Maybe I'll just leave you in the car and let the gas — "

You figure out Reles's play when the chatter of gunfire from an AK starts up from behind you. M43 rounds put holes in the car's windshield, making deadly little stars in the glass with each shot. The next rounds shatter the side and rear windows.

For a moment, you're sure you are shot. It's hard to breathe.

Agent Smith's hand is no longer on your neck. He slumps forward, draped across your back. His pistol thunks to the floor. There's a sound that hot, fast metal makes when it hits a body. You feel the vibration as each round tunnels through him. Smith doesn't scream as he goes. Just a soft grunt and his last hot breath escapes his slack jaws into your ear. It's as if Agent Smith softens and melts away into death.

Smith was human a moment ago. Now he's a sack of meat in what was once a decent suit.

Death is always a surprise, even when it's expected. It's awful when it's slow, but sometimes it's so lightning quick there's no transition time for the victim. A person is there and suddenly they are not. There's no time for Smith to process what's happening to him, no moment of clarity and noble last words. When death happens this quick, it makes you worry there's no meaning at all. Smith's erasure seems to carry no more significance to the universe than the death of a rabbit in the jaws of a coyote. Maybe less so. At least the rabbit sees the predator coming and has a chance to run.

You're under heavy, dead weight as the metal rain continues in short bursts. The shooter has moved on to other targets. By the screams, you can tell he's aiming to wound. You don't have to risk poking your head up. You know what he's doing. Reles must be in a high window in a house directly across the street from his own house. He's spreading the misery around, creating chaos.

Kill a man and he's down. Wound a man and two

others may risk their lives to save the fallen. The short bursts continue. The screams go on and on.

RT TO HUNT A MONSTER, YOU MUST BE ONE. TAKE THAT NIETZSCHE. @ASSASSINSPLAYBK

In your mind's eye, you picture knees exploding, feet turned to red mash and fingers lost. The regular cops will be pinned down. Pistols are useless against rifles at this range. Whoever's left of SWAT will be organizing, looking for a safe route from cover so they can outflank him. They'll be crouching behind engine blocks and calling for more backup, an LAPD helicopter and God.

They'll need the Medcat, an armored vehicle with four litters, to pull out the casualties. A Ballistic Engineered Armored Response Counter Attack Truck AKA a BearCat is also on the menu so SWAT can safely approach Reles's position.

You can't hear Reles laugh, but you'd bet anything he is laughing. He might even have an erection. Guys like him, whatever he does is about power. He works out hard to intimidate. He trains hard to make himself scarier. He victimizes girls and women. Behind the monster's mask, to feel such a need to be what he is, how incredibly weak

Reles must be. Under his suit of muscle, Reles is terrified all the time.

"Fear leads to anger. Anger leads to hate. Hate leads to suffering." Yoda was goddamned right. Beneath the anger is always fear.

The street will be filled with men and women in uniform trying to save themselves and each other under fire. Helping people is so hard. Hurting them is too easy.

If you were Reles, you'd have two Remington ACRs up in that high window. As soon as both mags on the Adaptive Combat Rifles clicked empty, you'd throw smoke and run, leaving the weapons behind, probably rigged with an IED if you had enough time to plan ahead. Maybe Reles will toss a grenade or two, as well. He doesn't seem to have any respect for his brothers and sisters in arms, but then, he was never really one of them. He's a maniac and a criminal who somehow managed to slip through the screening process.

You didn't really become a criminal until you were out of the military and the legit world had no more use for you. You remind yourself that you're very different from Reles. That's a good thing to try to remember because you know what happens next. When the police mount a counterattack, Reles will be long gone, but he'll leave behind plenty of toys to slow the cops down.

How many IEDs did Reles leave behind him to cover his retreat? How many feet of detcord trail through that house? How many decoy devices and spoilsport time bombs await anyone who tries to get to his position? He might even have a claymore waiting for his pursuers.

You would.

As soon as the shooting stops from the neighbor's house,

you push Agent Smith off you and out through the open door. He lands in the street with a wet smack. His left eye stares at the sky. His right eye points at you.

"Sorry, man." Staying low, you slip through the passenger side door. The keys to the handcuffs hang from Smith's belt. Your hands shake as you crawl into the driver's seat. The car keys are in the ignition.

Before the police can recover from the attack, you roar away as the first smoke bombs hit the pavement. Between the gas cloud behind them and the billowing smoke screen in front of them, both you and Reles have plenty of cover for your escape.

No police stand at the cordon. The civilians have run for their lives or they're cowering in clutches behind sparse cover. You hit the lights and sirens. It's a long time since you drove a cruiser under lights and sirens, except back then it was a Jeep. It feels good. With all the broken windows, the experience is weirdly familiar.

As you speed past, one of the strobes freezes Eleanor and Uri in light. In their terror, the old couple clutch each other.

The tires squeal as you tear around the back of the block, hoping to catch Reles on the run. You've got Agent John Smith's blood all over you and his 9 mm at the ready. Your weapons are in the trunk. You're on a righteous mission.

However, the universe doesn't care about what feels right. Indifferent to your need for vengeance, it's about the distance between stars and people. Nature is hot chemistry and cold physics. You are alone and Reles gets away.

You get away, too, because you think like him. You're the star of your movie. You're the hero. You tell yourself that you are not like Hank Reles. But somewhere, from far away — in the chasm between the fearful boy you were and the man you've become — there is an echo of doubt from a basement in Miami.

You slip out of character. Just for a moment, you let the mask fall. You aren't *you*, anymore.

I am. I am like Hank Reles.

Before you begin to weep, you reach for your rage. That's never far away. All you have to do is to think of Tia Marta with her hot iron. You summon the memory of the Bug Man of Surfside Beach. That memory is as ready as ever. You see him standing over you with his big mirrored aviator sunglasses. He asks, "Paper or plastic?" before slipping a bag over your head.

The sunglasses made him *look* like a bug, but he had an uncaring, insectile heart, too. As the bag slipped over your head — before the hot plastic clung to your face to take your air and thoughts away — you glimpsed your face in the mirrors concealing the Bug Man's eyes.

Yours is a little boy's face confronted with the truth of the universe too soon. That is the face of fear and helplessness and utter incomprehension.

The hate roars back.

You're powerful and righteous again. Your hate will lead to Reles's suffering. Knowing this, the little boy in the basement slips back into the dark, out of sight, back to Miami, swept away into history.

You are very much like Hank Reles. That's why you're the one to kill him.

RT HOW TO GET BLOOD OFF YOU.
@ASSASSINSPLAYBK

At the home of Legs Gabrielle, Sgt. Billy opens the back door. His eyes are wide as he takes you in.

"I know. It's a lot of blood but none of it's mine. The van is parked down the hill."

You remove your shoes so you don't track blood through the house. Sgt. Billy promises to run them under a hose out back and points you upstairs to a bedroom suite with a shower.

Big Denny told you once that, when covered with someone else's blood, it's best to shower with cold water first. "You want to keep the pores closed. People are filthy. Who knows what they've got or where they've been?"

You're not sure the cold water trick really works, but you scrub and shiver as long as you can stand it under a cold blast. You get all of Smith's blood off before you chance spinning the shower dial to hot. Soon the bathroom is steamed to a fog. You're still scrubbing when you hear the door open and there's a human figure beyond the fogged glass.

For a second, you're sure it must be Reles, as relentless as the devil. When you realize you aren't dead at the bottom of the shower yet, you hope it's Legs.

It's Sugar.

"Brought a towel for you."

"Thanks."

"You okay?"

"I will be."

"How do you know?"

"Experience. At least, that's how it's worked out so far. I expect that will continue until it doesn't."

"Did you see Detective Reles?"

"No. But it was him."

"How do you know?"

"Because of what he planned and how he slings bullets."

"It's all over the news. They're looking for you, too. Wolf Blitzer is on CNN calling Pacific Heights a war zone."

"War zones are everywhere, but usually they're confined to bedrooms and living rooms and kitchen tables. How many cops are dead?"

"Two. Plenty more injured. They aren't saying for sure yet."

"Thanks for the update. Will you excuse me while I clean up?"

"Sure. Go ahead." Sugar doesn't leave.

"I need some time here."

"Take your time."

"What do you want?"

"Tell me…about what you do…what's the worst thing you ever did?"

"Why do you want to know, Sugar?"

"Maybe so I can feel better about the things I've had to do."

You let the hot water wash over you for a minute before answering.

There's a lot of competition for the worst thing you've ever done. You pick the first thing that comes to mind. You tell Sugar about the time you killed the Ghost.

RT SMART HIT MEN WORK ON AN EMPTY STOMACH. @ASSASSINSPLAYBK

The Ghost moved like an old man but he was really only fifty or so. This was the first job you pulled for The Machine. Big Denny said you had to make your bones so the boss, Vincent Lima, would know you were solid.

When you came back from Iraq via Germany, you'd scrounged for jobs but no one would hire you. Meanwhile, Big Denny had a car and wasn't worrying about how to pay for his next meal. He said the hours were easy and it was better than living on the street. You'd done plenty of that already and didn't want to go back.

Big Denny drove you out to a shack in the middle of nowhere. Wantage, New Jersey. He parked by the side of the road and you both watched the place for a while. Plastic flamingos crammed the front yard. The maple tree out front was all wind chimes. Concentric metal and plastic rings twisted hypnotically in the breeze. The mailbox was topped with a wooden sculpture of two men on either end of a little saw that moved back and forth when the wind was just right. A pink, hand-painted sign read: Yard Art 4 SALE.

"It's a guy selling a bunch of crap. What business does the Spanish mob have way out here?"

"Their business."

"C'mon, man. I can't kill some guy without knowing why."

Big Denny shook his head. "That's not how this works. You only get to know what you need to know. It's just like the Army, Jesus. Did they let you do a lot of thinking for yourself?"

"No. They didn't, but if I'm going to do this, I need to know he's a bad guy who deserves it."

Big Denny put a paw on your shoulder and stared into your eyes. "The Ghost is a bad guy who deserves it."

"You know this for sure?"

"Valid. I know it."

"Fine. Gimme the throwaway gun."

"The boss says no."

"What?"

"Sorry, buddy. The assignment comes straight from Vincent but Jimmy added a twist."

"Who the hell is Jimmy?"

"That would be the boss's son."

"Of course."

"You gotta go in without a gun or a knife to do it."

"Jimmy doesn't want to hire me at all, does he?"

"I vouched for you, but Jimmy's got a hard on for Cubans. He says if you do the job as ordered, you're in and they'll start you off with nice bank and a no-show job in construction. If I have to do the job, you're out. You can't no-show on the hit, man."

230

You stared at your oldest friend for a long minute. "You mean if I don't do the job, you're supposed to kill me, too, right?"

"Jesus!" Big Denny put on his hurt feelings look with puppy dog eyes. He looked like a scolded pug. "After all we've been through together, you can ask that?"

"Denny. Dude."

"Yeah, okay, I'm supposed to do you if you don't do him, but you know I wouldn't. You'd have to disappear, though. It would be a whole…thing, you know. Let's not make this a big thing. No complications, no danger. You Scooby Doo the Ghost, we go get pancakes. There's a great pancake place in West Orange on the way back."

"I don't want to go get pancakes after ending somebody!"

"Well, Christ! Then you box up yours for later, drama king. I come all the way out here? I want pancakes. Now get out of the car and do him. Remember, I vouched for you. Maybe nothing good happens to me if you don't pan out. You ever think of that?"

You got out of the car and looked around. The metal circles within circles twisted faster as a cold breeze wafted over you. You shivered, but you were sweating, too.

Big Denny rolled down his window. "He lives alone. I'll honk if somebody shows up but nobody's going to show up. One other thing. You're supposed to make it look like an accident. But you're supposed to make a statement."

"What does that mean?"

"A statement."

"Yeah?"

"You know…like…drama…like…I don't fuckin' know. Do what you can. It's from Jimmy. He's a little off."

Before you could argue further, Big Denny De Molina rolled up the window, locked the door and waved you on.

You walked to the front door and knocked. You jumped when a cat in the front window leapt away. You hadn't realized it was there until you caught the movement in the corner of your eye.

The Ghost came to the door. You had assumed he got the name from being some kind of spy worthy of the moniker. The guy who answered the door wasn't the sort who looked like he could pass through borders and assume multiple identities. He stood at the door in his pyjamas, bent at the waist and neck and leaning on an IV pole.

"Hey," you said.

A moment passed. "Well?"

"I wanna buy all your flamingos. My boss is having a birthday. I need forty-seven. He's forty-seven."

"That right?" The Ghost peered around you to look at Big Denny in the car. He frowned. "You drove all the way out from New York for my flamingos?"

"Yes. Yes, I did."

He looked you up and down. "Bullshit. You've come to kill me."

"I — "

"Come on in. Let's get it over with."

RT WHERE TO HIDE THE #GUN. @ASSASSINSPLAYBK

The Ghost sat in a plaid chair the cat had scratched to shreds. The television was a huge old set with rabbit ears pulling in a ragged signal from FOX News.

"Well?"

You stood in the Ghost's house and looked around. No pictures of his loved ones. No hint of what he did for the mob that got him in trouble. You don't know what you expected, but never this.

"This is a test, isn't it?" you asked.

"More for me than you, I hope. What's a matter? First time?"

You didn't answer and his face fell. "Oh, shit. They sent me a rookie. That's less respect than I was hoping for."

"I've killed people," you said.

The Ghost looked you up and down and smirked. "Self-defense, though, right? Not like this? Not a sick guy in a chair." He nodded at his IV pole and the tube snaking into the back of his wrist. He tapped the pole with a finger. "Kidneys. Never had a family or enough friends to scrounge up a spare kidney for a transplant."

"That sucks."

"Yup. But now it's harder for you like this, isn't it? You're wondering why they don't just let me die in peace."

"Why aren't they?"

"Whaddayou? The Ghost of Christmas Past? I'm the Ghost of Your Future, you little shit. I ben a *bastid*, okay?"

"Oh."

"Yeah. Oh. And now I've got a wet behind the ears wannabe assassin. You'll probably fuck it up. You look like a fuck up."

"And this is why you have no friends."

He smiled. "A good, quick death would be better than fading away. I'm sick of sittin' there in the clinic, going for dialysis. I'm not much of a reader. Other people read while they get the dialysis. I sit there watchin' the pretty nurses and wish I was twenty years younger." He sighed and stared at you. "So on a cold autumn day in Wantage, New Jersey, you show up at my door on the last day of my life to do me the favor of a quick death. Feels like I'm doin' *you* the favor, fuck up."

"I'm starting to think I should turn around and let you die slow, Ghost. You're too rude to die quick."

He laughed at the joke. Then he laughed at you. Then he farted loudly and got up abruptly. "Outta my way! I haven't had a decent shit in days and if you aren't going to do it, let me poop out a present for you to take with you, back to New York."

He disappeared into the bathroom but left the door ajar.

The cat looked at you as if to say, "Well?"

You spotted the Metamucil on the kitchen counter.

234

You kicked the door open and he sat on the toilet with a revolver pointed at your gut. You grabbed for it. The Ghost failed to get off a shot. The cylinder couldn't turn in your grip. You twisted it away from him. "Dude!"

"Always keep a back-up gun behind the toilet tank, kid. If you're going to last in this business, learn your craft, for Christ sake! Be observant. Be a smart ninja."

"Any last words?"

"Don't give assholes the chance to say any last words. They'll pop you if you play by the rules."

"Okay. That it?"

"Why are you doing this, kid? I don't think your heart's in it."

You looked around his bathroom. The tub had never been scrubbed. The paint flaked off the walls. Whatever he'd done, it sure didn't look like it paid. "Why did you do whatever you did for the mob, Ghost?"

He smiled. "Wantage. I live in Wantage. I'm filled with wantage."

You unscrewed the cap off the Metamucil canister and told him to tip his head back and open wide. He cooperated. You poured the orange powder in and he started to cough immediately.

His saliva turned the powder to sludge too slowly so you poured in a little water from the sink. Not so much for him to swallow. Just enough that the sludge expands in his throat and cuts off his airway. He died thrashing, bare assed on the toilet.

You thought you killed him. You sort of did, though, a week later, the newspaper reported that he'd died of a heart attack. His real name was Leonard Meinhof. The coroner's report didn't mention more details, but the home care nurse who found Ghost told the newspaper that she'd found the man's face eaten by his cat.

You told yourself you'd done the dying man a favor. Back in Denny's car, you realized the wheel gun from behind the toilet tank was empty. Ghost had done you the favor. It still wasn't self-defense, but you'd thought yourself a smart ninja for using a common household medication for constipation to your advantage. The Ghost had made it easier for you.

"Congratulations," Denny said. "Cherry's broken. You're in and the pancakes are on me."

"Waffles."

"Whatever."

"Denny?"

"Yeah?"

"I'm in, right?"

"Balls deep."

"What did he do?"

"What? The Ghost?"

"What did he *do*, Den? Between us. He's a bad guy. You said it. I Scooby Doo'd the Ghost, just like you said. I'm in. So? What's his deal?"

Big Denny laughed. "No fuckin' clue. Welcome to The Machine, Jesus."

"You said he deserved it! You sonofabitch!"

Denny just shrugs and laughs and you promise you'll get back at him.

"Yeah, sure," he says. "Someday. Everybody swears they'll get even someday. Nobody gets even a little bit of justice."

The waffles in West Orange did taste good, but by the time Denny got you as far as East Orange he pulled over

236

so you could puke in a ditch. You were still so mad at him you refused to get out. Big Denny was still trying to push you out of his car when you yelled, "A little bit of justice, bitch!" and threw up all over him.

RT CONFESSION IS GOOD FOR THE PROSECUTING ATTORNEY. @ASSASSINSPLAYBK

You've never confessed all the details to anyone but Big Denny. Sugar was the wrong person to open up to. She stands outside the shower, laughing. It's not a funny story. At least, it isn't a funny story to you.

Legs pokes her head in. "Now's not the time for fun and games, kiddies. Everyone out of the pool. You'll get your fingers all pruney."

You poke your head out of the shower stall and you and Sugar say together, "We didn't do anything."

Legs rolls her eyes.

Sugar gives you a hard look. This morning, Sugar does not look sweet but you figure PTSD takes many forms. For a girl you found kidnapped, beaten and threatened in a cage, she's actually doing remarkably well.

Legs grabs the towel, throws it at you and pulls Sugar out the door. After you dry yourself off, you discover Sgt. Billy has retrieved clothes for you from the van.

You're still getting your shirt on when Legs pounds on

the door. "We need to talk, Jesus!"

You tell her to come in and, as she rushes in with Sugar behind her, you turn away to finish buttoning your shirt, hiding your scars again.

"I'm sorry," Legs says. "I didn't mean to embarrass you."

"It's okay." Your tone tells her it's not okay.

Sugar puts a soft hand on your shoulder. "It is okay, though. Scars mean life. Everybody's got them, seen and unseen." She buttons your top two buttons for you, smiles and knots your tie. An Oxford knot. She's done this before. She pats your cheek and sits on the bed. "Who taught you to be ashamed of your scars? The person who gave them to you?"

"No. Tia Marta liked scars too much. She enjoyed giving them. Skin without a scratch was an invitation to her."

"So? Who made you feel bad?"

You smile. "The truth is, it was a girl from Princeton. In the Army, scars were a macho bullshit sort of badge of honor. But once I was out…I don't go swimming in public pools. Let's leave it at that."

"No," Sugar says. "Tell us about the girl from Princeton."

Legs moves to stand by the bed. "I need to talk about Reles."

"Wait," Sugar says. "Let him tell it. He tells good stories."

You sigh. "Not much to tell. I was self-conscious, especially about the burns. When I was dating, I tried to stay clothed. Even making love in the dark…well…a woman putting her hands on my bare back…you know.

You can feel thick scars and next thing, they want to turn on the light."

"Is that what the girl did?"

"Something like that. We were alone in her dorm and we'd already been making out pretty heavy. She...well, you know...she got to feeling pretty good."

"You got her off, you mean?" Sugar asks.

"Ehm. Yeah. I turn off the light and now that she's achieved some satisfaction, we're basically two strangers in the dark. I thought I knew where this was going, but now that she's had her...er...climax, she doesn't seem too concerned about mine."

"Women can be such bitches sometimes," Sugar says.

You clear your throat. "Um...anyway, things slow down and she's smoking beside me in the dark and she's gotten quiet. I've made my move and I thought we were already on a trajectory, you know? A glide path where we land at a happy airport. Instead, she's put us in a holding pattern."

"What'd you do?" Sugar asks.

"I start talking to her about her life at Princeton. She's already tired of college guys and she's thinking about maybe becoming a professor or traveling more, but she doesn't know what she really wants. Eventually, she finishes her smoke and it looks pretty bleak."

"And you've got blue balls," Sugar says. She smiles and licks her lips in a way that makes you need to look away.

The licking thing reminds you of the old lady, Eleanor. Also, the fact that Sugar is a submissive prostitute makes you squeamish about her advances. Legs is smart and funny. Smart, powerful women are more to your taste. You wish it was Legs looking at you and licking her lips that way.

"Anyway," you say. "The girl gets off the bed and tells me to take off my shirt and pants. I start to get nervous, but she keeps the room dark. She opens up a tiny fridge and in a moment she's back with whipped cream in a can."

"Oh, yeah!" Sugar says.

"For me, it's more like 'Oh, no!' She unbuttoned my shirt and put cold whipped cream on my nipples. I should be thinking about the sex, but I'm just hoping she doesn't touch the crucifixion scar on my chest. She'll either think I'm part of some Catholic cult or — "

"She'll think it's ugly," Sugar says.

"Hey!" Legs says sharply.

"Yeah. No. She's right," you admit. "So I'm feeling nervous and I start trying to get the attention back on her. I start talking...well...heh. I start rambling, really. An Army buddy had this patter he used on girls. He started talking philosophy with them, about sexual freedom and being your own autonomous person and whatnot. I was nervous. I don't know what the hell I was doing. When she stops licking my nipples, I know I've fucked up."

"She felt the scar, huh?" Legs asks.

"No. I was talking about the short life and deep thoughts of Albert Camus. I'd read all about him. I was trying to pick up girls at Princeton, for God's sake! I wanted to impress them. Some of them liked the uniform well enough, but when I talked, I felt too stupid to share their air. A guy named Dallas suggested the way to a smart girl's heart was to talk about Albert Camus. I'd read his stories. The novels were short and better than his philosophy, really. But I'd never stepped into a classroom. I'd never heard his name...well, I'd never heard his name spoken by someone who knew how to pronounce it. Dallas steered me wrong. I pronounced it like '*Kay-muss.*' It's pronounced '*Ka-moo!*'"

"So?" Sugar wouldn't have cared. That fact makes you like her a little more.

"What happened?" Legs asks.

"She thought my mistake was hilarious. She started giggling. Then she sat up quick and turned on the light. And there I am, naked with nothing but three columns of whipped cream to hide me."

"*Three?* Oh. Not three nipples." Sugar has a wicked smile.

"It's another of those stories that should be funny, I guess. Except that's when she started screaming. You two ladies are the first to see my scars since then."

Legs smiles, too, but not unkindly. Still, she's a comic. If Reles doesn't kidnap and kill her first, this story is going to be retold onstage in a club in Denver to a roaring drunk audience someday. You're guessing that Legs will assume the role of the hapless naked goof in the bed and the embarrassment will be over an appendix scar. It won't be as good, but she'll find a way to amp it up and sell it for laughs.

"Sorry that happened to you," Legs says. "But we need to talk about how you're going to track down Reles."

You were about to explain how you need to use her as bait. Instead, Sugar's cell rings. She hands you the phone. It's Hank Reles.

He tells you to meet him at your abandoned apartment over Big in Japan.

"The FBI are sitting on that place. That's why I'm not there."

"I've taken care of the FBI. That's why I'm here."

"What does that mean?"

"You can imagine."

"What if I don't come?" you say. "It would be easier to just call the cops on your ass."

"You won't. What if I get away again? I could just disappear. Got that all planned out. Then one day I could resurface. You'll know when that day happens because Legs Gabrielle, my fair lady, will have disappeared off the face of the Earth. Don't worry, though. I'll keep that bitch in a little dog cage, alive for a while, anyway. She doesn't know how to behave yet, but I can crate her, train her, bring her to heel and rub her nose in it."

"I see your point."

"Don't get cute, Jesus. If the cops get to me before you do, you'll never find out what happened to your mother."

"I don't — "

"*After* Surfside Beach."

"She's — "

"Maritza Diaz. You remember Surfside Beach, don't you? I'll bet you do."

"When do we meet?"

"As soon as you get here."

"On my way."

RT THE FBI HAS OVER 85,000 ACTIVE MISSING PERSONS CASES. @ASSASSINSPLAYBK

In the United States, about 1,800 people disappear every day. You've seen stats as high as 2,300 a day. Where all the people go is a mystery. Where are all the people kicked out of their homes in Detroit, for instance? Where could they all go?

Dallas, the fat pickup artist and Albert Camus fan, told you the missing persons phenomenon comprised crazy people, teenage runaways and black ops renditions, but the renditions were really a cover up for alien abduction. On further consideration, you shouldn't have been taking any dating advice from Dallas.

Many of the missing are found or wander back home on their own, but the FBI has 85,000 active missing persons cases. Maritza Diaz, your mother, is one of them. You looked for her yourself, of course. Later, you accepted that she drowned that day at Surfside Beach and never got a proper burial.

Now the hope that you aren't alone in the world is back.

Hope burns bright, even in dark places. That's what speeds you back to the little parking lot behind Big in Japan and up the back stairs. Your hope dims quickly.

You find the first FBI agent at the bottom of the stairs. He's nailed to the wall: pinned, dead and staring, arms outstretched. Hank Reles counts a nail gun among his toys. There's a big knife still sticking out of his gut. It's a crude crucifixion and a message to you. The agent didn't take two or three days to die, though. The blood streaming down his face isn't from a crown of thorns. He was beaten about the skull, just like Chill.

You point your SIG up the stairs. "Reles? You up there?"

"Yeah, we're here."

"Who is we?"

"We is me and my new buddy, Agent Caruthers. C'mon up. Don't worry. He's disarmed and having a nap."

"How do I know you won't shoot? You've already tried to kill me."

"Took out your guard and covered your escape from the Federal Bureau of Injustice, didn't I?" He laughs. "Would you feel better if you knew I was only following orders?"

"Did the order come from Big Denny?"

"Shit, no. Gaston wants you dead. Wouldn't really surprise me if a bunch of other people want you on the dirt side of the grass, too."

"Common problem. We share that."

"Funny you're so hard to kill. Guess you got toughened up young, huh?"

"Why do you want to talk now?"

"C'mon, Jesus! You killed Tia Marta for me, so I owe

you for that much."

"What?"

"What I said."

"I'm intrigued. I am not reassured. Go on. Why the big light show for the cops?"

"No, stupid. For Gaston. If I follow orders, he gives me a free ride out of here on a yacht. It's always good to do what Gaston tells you to do. He's a rich guy."

"What do you want to know, Reles? You didn't call me here for gits and shiggles."

"Heh. I've got everybody looking for me thanks to you. Maybe I wanna see the man who screwed up my shit, eye to eye. You want to know what I want? How about this? How long did you have to beat on Mueller before he gave me up?"

"Oh, that. All I had to do was say please."

"Heh. He was a bitch. You want to know where Maritza is now? Let's talk like men. I want something from you. You got a gun. I got a gun. But what I have to say will need a face to face."

You take out your phone and select the camera. You crawl on your belly down the narrow hallway until you can reach the bottom corner of the door. You snap a quick picture and pull back.

The tactic is half recon but mostly it's a test. The picture shows Reles standing behind a guy in a suit. The guy in the suit is slumped in a chair. The hostage does not fit Gaston Bekhti's description. The hostage who isn't really a hostage trick had to be ruled out first.

As to the test, it's important to note that Reles didn't try to shoot you through the wall when you took the picture. He's just standing there, his gun at his side. Also of note,

Detective Reles is shirtless. This is a significant detail. He's not just showing off the rock hard abs and slabs of muscle. He's letting you see his scars.

As you enlarge the photo on your screen, you gasp. Your scars are like wings across your back. The raised crescents of iron burns spread across Reles's chest. You've seen that burn pattern once before, across a boy's chest.

What name do you go by, muchacho? Like dialogue from an old Western.

He'd asked you that. Back in the cafe across from the comedy club, he didn't simply ask your name. He was asking what your alias was. You should have asked him the same question.

"*Darren?*"

"Darren Hill from Sarasota. You didn't recognize me before, but I guess we didn't know each other very long. You were my replacement."

"I thought you were dead. And you weren't built like the Hulk then. And mostly we were in the dark."

"Last time I talked to you," Reles says, "you didn't speak English."

You step into the doorway, pistol ready. He sinks, his gun is against the unconscious man's head. The FBI agent is a human shield. Kind of ironic since Agent Smith was your shield.

"Hi, Jesus. Funny that we were kids together and now here we are again. Reunion time." He points his pistol at you. You might be able to clip him, but if he fires, he'll definitely hollow you out.

You drop the SIG.

As soon as your weapon thunks to the floor, Reles pushes the chair over and the FBI agent falls flat. His neck shouldn't move that way, or that far to the side. It's loose, like the bones have melted. You watch the agent's chest, but of course it doesn't move.

You fell for the false hostage trick, after all.

RT A GOOD CHOKEHOLD TAKES YOU OUT FAST. THINK BLOOD, NOT AIR. @ASSASSINSPLAYBK

Reles orders you to take out your cell phone.

With shaking hands, you do as you're told. You went with the Android because you can take the battery out of an Android. iPhones are easier to trace. You wish you had an iPhone with you now. The cops could be surrounding the place, rescuing you. Ha! No. SWAT would shoot you both.

"Call Legs," he says.

"It won't do you any good."

"Call her or I'll kneecap you and then you'll call her anyway, but crying hard."

You have to agree with his logic so you dial the number that might just save your life. That's extremely unlikely, of course, but when you're dealing with a crazed stalker who also happens to be a cop killer, it's important to make them feel loved.

He takes a step closer, menacing and meaning business but not so close you can make a desperate lunge and play hero. He picks up your gun and gestures with the SIG to make you hurry up so he can speak with Legs Gabrielle. Maybe he'll lure her out of hiding. Maybe he'll shoot you between the eyes and taunt her.

You thought the movie reel of your life would flash by in your last moments. You didn't want to endure that because, frankly, your childhood was brutal and filled with death. However, your brain doesn't rehash all that. Instead, you get one of those short, independent films that plays in art cinemas that nobody sees. You get the most recent replay of the brutality, death and stupid mistakes that landed you at this place and time. Like the rest of your life, if not for the funny bits, the replay would be too much for your heart to take. It's hard to say which part of your life weighs heaviest on you. Too late to make corrections now.

The childhood stuff happened to you and none of that was your fault. The little film that runs through your head now? This is your fault. It's a clever and funny story, but mostly desperate. Call it *The Dumb Assassin's Playbook* by Jesus Diaz, the bullshit artist who died because he believed his own hype. You thought you were so smart, which — more irony and embarrassment — is a key component of winding up with a target on your forehead.

"Now!" the big man roars.

Push that button. But don't expect escape. No one escapes the past. You hope to die and be reborn for another shot at a long boring life among kind people.

You take a deep breath, squeeze your eyes tight and three...two...one...you hit *Send. Is this all there is?* Time to find out.

You open your mouth, but not to speak.

The mines you hid in the dead air conditioning unit explode and the cave-in takes the roof. The ceiling collapses under the weight of three tons of steel. Detective Hank Reles isn't just killed. He is erased. The air conditioner squashes him flat and keeps going through the second floor. It crashes through, all the way to the ground floor and the basement.

Monsters shouldn't die so quickly, but you went with the only play you had left.

The concussive wave slams you back, but fortunately, your mouth was open and you remembered not to hold your breath. Anticipating an explosion, that's anyone's natural instinct, but that's not the smart ninja's play. If you had held your breath that close to the explosion, your lungs would have popped like balloons and your first and last clue you were dead would have been the taste of blood. An open mouth lessens the effect of the wall of air that just got displaced, too, but the headache is still epic. It feels like your head is trapped in a vice and your brain is a throbbing, aching thing slamming around the inside of your skull trying to get out of the dark.

But you don't die. Instead, you're trapped in the present tense, living and dying in the awful now. You claw at the door frame at the edge of the apartment so you won't get sucked down the hole. The choking dust and debris hangs in the air. What's left of your futon is on fire as it slides into the expanding hole in the middle of the floor. Your ears ring with a whine that goes on and on. You stumble to the stairs and lean on the railing, feeling your way through a cloud of brown dust.

When you emerge from the building at the bottom of the rear stairs, you can't stop coughing. The dizziness consumes. It feels like your brain has slipped a gear. The mines you got from the Chicago gig were your trump card. You thought you'd use the explosives if Big Denny De Molina's enforcers ever found you. Sometimes it pays to have lots of enemies.

Sugar pulls up in Legs Gabrielle's car. She steps out and beams a smile at you. She's wearing a splashy red party dress. You're still coughing and dizzy, but seeing her makes you smile. You wave to let her know you're okay. She waves back. You feel like you've saved your little sister from the wolf. Another monster's dead. One more monster to find.

"Paper or plastic?" A voice speaks from behind you. A plastic bag slips over your head. Somehow, the Bug Man of Surfside Beach has found you again. A sinewy forearm wraps around your windpipe as you gasp for breath.

Nightmares live.

The building is on fire. Smoke and sirens fill the air. Your air won't last long enough for any help to arrive.

"You could have been a king," the Bug Man says. "In another life, you could have come with us, been one of us. You could have been drinking beer on a yacht and heading to South America. We could have lived like gods in Uruguay. We could have lived on sangria on ice and women on tap and Viagra and poppers forever. But you killed Marta and Hank! You took my best from me, you thieving, filthy little pig."

Ah. Right. You stole the Bug Man's Armani suits when you fled North, too. But the Bug Man took your mother and brother. Tia Marta took your childhood. Worse than all that, the Bug Man is directly behind you, killing you as he promised. Hank Reles took your pistol. Your hope for

vengeance is dying as fast as you are.
    Seconds left.

RT REVENGE IS BEST SERVED WHILE YOU'RE STILL YOUNG ENOUGH TO ENJOY IT. @ASSASSINSPLAYBK

You screwed up the future, but the future is a tiny thing now. Soon, you will no longer exist.

Desperate to play for time and break his grip, you slump to the ground, letting your dead weight pull him down. He doesn't break the chokehold. Instead, he follows you down like a pro. Your head slams into the pavement.

Stars. You see stars, darting back and forth and getting brighter as your vision becomes a dark tunnel. The tunnel gets longer. Through the plastic, at the end of the tunnel, you see a figure in red. Sugar is coming. The only light at the end of your tunnel is the color of blood.

"Your mother made it to shore, you know, Jesus." The Bug Man grunts from the effort. He's older now, of course, but still plenty strong enough. He's sure he's won. You can feel his breath coming hard and fast, crinkling the plastic at your ear. Your dying flame of rage leaps higher when the Bug Man says, "I made Maritza one of my girls. She didn't last long. She didn't give up like you. Some women have too much spirit."

You flail weakly, one hand trying to pry his fist open. If you could get just one finger in your palm, you could peel him off you. But the Bug Man knows how to choke a man out. He's no doubt had lots of practice on boys and girls.

You can't do it.

You can't get away.

You can't.

Your other hand closes on the hilt of the switchblade in your sock. The Bug Man screams as you plunge the blade into his crotch.

His arm isn't wrapped around your throat anymore. You twist away and pull the hot plastic off your face and gasp. That first full breath is like a tall glass of ice water in the desert. When you turn to look the Bug Man in the eyes and slash his throat open, that's even better than that first full breath.

It is no surprise at all that the Bug Man of Surfside Beach must be the elusive Gaston Bekhti. As soon as you knew that Detective Hank Reles was really Darren Hill from Sarasota, you guessed the rest. Sex slavery, snuff films and all manner of depravity require networks and infrastructure and providers. Monsters, in other words.

Blood pumps from the Bug Man's throat in spurts. Each geyser of blood is a little lower with each beat of his stone heart. His eyes are still furious.

Beat.

Beat.

Beat...beat...

His eyes are glass.

You're covered in blood. You can't help but smile. The Bug Man was once your god. He made you what you are.

It was he and Tia Marta who decided if and when you would eat, when and how much you would suffer. They threatened death each day you were trapped in the basement. Rather than graduate from the basement to become one of his soldiers, you slew your god and his kingdom has fallen.

No one really escapes their past but maybe you can change your future.

You roll to your back, breathing hard, waiting for your head to clear. Sugar is crying. Her thick mascara drains down her face in black trails.

"It's okay." You hold out your hand for Sugar to help you to your feet. If she gets you to the car, in a few minutes, all this will be a dot in the rearview mirror.

Sugar holds out her hand but she's not reaching for you. There's a Ruger LCP 380 in her fist. The pistol's frame is hot pink. Sugar Cane does not cry for you. You twist away as she fires twice. Two rounds rip through your side. Getting shot hurts, like you're on fire.

Reles knew so much about you and now you know why. Sugar must have heard you prowling around Oswald's house. She locked herself in the cage and tore her dress and smacked her face against the cage bars.

You fell for the false hostage trick, after all. Twice. Sugar Cane is another Tia Marta.

You want to talk to her. You want to air accusations and hear explanations. You never will. Sugar Cane's dress blossoms a deeper red. Her jaw drops. Her bright eyes dull. Her pink pistol drops from her slack hand. She drops to the hot pavement.

RT WHEN YOUR HIT MAN HAS WARM FEELINGS, HE'S HIGH OR ON FIRE. @ASSASSINSPLAYBK

You lie between two corpses and you're about to bleed out, the third sack of meat. You will no longer exist. Surprise. You aren't surprised. You should have become a bus driver or a professional salsa dancer or…well….just about anything else besides a guy who lives by the gun.

Big Denny De Molina looms above you, shaking his head. "What happened to you, man? You forgot where we came from."

Close your eyes. Let it all go away. Hope for the best. Expect oblivion. If not oblivion, maybe you'll see Chill in heaven. That would be far out and groovy. You can dig it. More likely, you'll wake up in hell, burning with all your deserving victims.

You feel numb. Death can't be far from here.

Open your eyes. Big Denny points his pistol your way. You somehow manage to lift the knife, which now seems to weigh about seventy pounds. Denny smirks and kicks it away. The knife spins away in slow motion. Denny steps closer. Then he steps on your forearm and pins you. You can't move and you've got no fight left.

Fight? Fight is a cold thing far away. Fight is a distant star. It will take eons for the light from Fight to reach Earth. By then you'll be skeleton dust and worm shit.

You look up at Denny and your eyes are so wet, it's as if you're looking up at him through water. This isn't the death scene you were hoping for. You aren't Jimmy Cagney in *White Heat* screaming, "Top of the world, ma!" in defiance. You wanted to be a hero. You hoped you'd have time to balance out the pain and find redemption. Instead, you're drowning in self-pity. You're helpless.

Big Denny fires and fires and fires until the gun clicks empty. With every shot, Gaston Bekhti's body shakes and shudders beside you.

You close your eyes. Strong arms pick you up. Gently, you are carried away.

An old memory surfaces, perhaps your earliest memory. You are on a burning beach in Cuba. Your legs are very tired and your bare feet are too hot in the sand. You dance to ease the heat. You hold your arms up, waiting, hoping. You are tiny. The sunlight dazzles.

Someone picks you up and carries you away. You close your eyes, relieved to be held and cared for. A wisp of long hair caresses your cheek. It must have been your mother. Goodbye, Maritza.

You hear voices but it's as if the words echo down a long tube. You don't understand what they are saying, but the tones are soothing. You think of the good people in your life and you wish them well. You hope Skunk stays righteous and carries on Chill's legacy of protecting people. You wish Berb all the best and you're so sorry you couldn't save Jeremy. You hope Sgt. Billy understands you love him. He was one of the few constants in your life, at least for a while.

You want them all to understand that with every action, you were doing the best you could at the time. First you were just trying to survive. Later, you tried to redeem yourself. You tell yourself you had a rough start, but you ended where you did for reasons that were your own. You forgave yourself for failing too easily.

You hope Legs Gabrielle gets every award and reward she so rightly deserves in Hollywood. It's a town famous for building up stars for everyone to worship. This place is also infamous for wishing upon falling stars, delighting in their crash to Earth.

When all these feelings flood in, you know you must be high. When you were addicted to Vicodin, you were full of benevolent feelings like this. Whatever is pumping through your blood and brain, the drug has emptied the word *hate* of all meaning.

You struggle to open your eyes. Tile ceiling. A monitor beeps along, steady and regular as your heart.

I am not dead.

You are back.

Jesus is resurrected.

RT LIFE IS A TRAIN THAT HITS THE END OF THE LINE WITHOUT BRAKES. @ASSASSINSPLAYBK

Big Denny De Molina sits in the chair beside the hospital bed, his chin on his chest and fast asleep.

Surprise! You are not dead or in federal custody. It hurts to laugh.

Big Denny startles, raises his huge head, and looks your way. A slow smile spreads across his face.

"The enemy of my enemy is my friend, huh?" Your throat is dry. Your voice comes in a rasp. "But our common enemy is dead now. Why didn't you let me bleed out? I'm getting too old for repeated beatings, if that's what you saved me for."

Denny shrugs. "You saved me from the basement, Jesus, from Tia Marta and the Bug Man. I forgive you for the misunderstanding in New York."

"What? You found Jesus?" This time, you don't pronounce it like your name. You say, "Gee-zuzz."

"I finally found you. I found Bekhti's boat first. I was stakin' that out. Figured if I'd followed him around long enough, you'd show up and we could kill him together, just like old times."

"How many houses do I have to blow up to give you the idea I want out? Did I forget to leave a memo? What? Does The Machine require two weeks' notice?"

He laughs. "Look at you. Makes me sick, seeing you go all Hollywood like this, all shot up and still trying to take on the world alone. What you get for hanging out with the swells without me, all fancy and shit. You was never meant for that world, man. People change, but nobody changes so much as you'd need to change to hang out with a chick like Legs Gabrielle. Who do you think you are?"

"I dunno, man. That's the problem."

Legs Gabrielle…you'll never see her again. Once again you've met the perfect woman and, again, the perfect woman is not for you. How many times must the same lesson be repeated until it is learned?

Denny leans in, watching your eyes get wet. "You okay, buddy? You need more painkillers? Bedpan? Hankie? Sponge bath?"

There aren't enough painkillers in the world. Shake it off, genius. "How is it you showed up at my back door, Denny? You follow Bekhti?"

"I wish. Didn't work out that way. Smith told me the FBI staked out that dump you were living in, but Smith didn't think you'd be stupid enough to go back there for any reason."

"But you thought I'd be stupid enough."

"Yeah. I had one of my guys keep an eye on the place." When he catches your look, he shrugs. "Dude! Smith was dirty. Everything is available for a price. Anyway, when my guy spotted Reles going in, they called me. I knew you'd show up. I left a comfortable seat watching Bekhti's boat just in time to save your life. And you're welcome, by the way."

"Uh…*gracias.*"

He makes the sign of the cross your way. "And now you're free of the Bug Man. Go in peace, bro."

But nothing is ever that easy. You've lived too long in this world to expect an easy ending. Forgiveness isn't enough. "What else, Denny?"

"What else, what else?"

"For starters, where am I and what's this gonna cost me?"

"You're in a private clinic."

"Private. Sounds pricey. Where?"

"Rosarito."

"Where?"

"Mexico."

"How?"

"Gaston has a very nice yacht. We borrowed the boat and his crew. Sorry you slept through the trip. Heavy sedation will do that. I got you fixed up in LA. Then I got you out."

"And me without my passport and no travel insurance. Gee. I could get in trouble, couldn't I?"

"You'll have a new passport soon. New identity. Jesus Diaz and Dr. J.D. Fix are dead."

"Deep down, I knew those guys couldn't last."

"Well, we're almost even, but you owe me for the two guys you killed at Oswald's. They were freelancers, but still, it's the principle of the thing. They worked for me and now I gotta pay off a couple of widows and make things smooth."

"Knew this was gonna cost me big. Those guys were

careless and impolite, Denny. Now what do you want from me?"

He shrugs. "Tit for tat. Quid for quo. I scratch your back, you shave mine. You know…capitalism. That's life. You owe me. That's America."

"We're in Mexico."

"That's the bonus of being an American, Jesus. No matter where we go, we act like we're home. I always carry a little bit of Jersey with me." He pats his jacket over the left armpit where his shoulder holster bulges.

"Yeah. I know the rule. You owe, you pay. But those freelancers came at me heavy, Denny."

"Yeah, well, they weren't my best operators. But you'll do, if you're smart enough to take the job I'm offering you."

"Look at you, all grown up and talking like a boss."

"You haven't been keeping track of what's going on in New York, have you?"

"You're the boss?"

"Nah. Not quite. A boss. Not the boss. I still have people to answer to, just like always. Besides, nobody calls nobody 'boss', anymore. Get some class."

"Yeah? What do they call you now?"

"Sir."

"Oh. No shit?"

"Yeah."

"What do you want for the guys who came after me and were rude about it?"

"Lily."

"What?"

"You heard me."

"I haven't seen Lily since — "

"Since you helped her walk away with my money."

"It wasn't yours at the time."

"It is now."

"I thought she was going to Spain to check out some paintings."

"She was in Spain, then Prague. I don't know where Prague is. Then she was in London. Now she's in New Orleans."

"Doing what?"

"You'll find out."

"Yeah? I'm shot and we're quits. She's my ex, man. I have no special powers when it comes to Lily. Not anymore. I don't think I ever had special influence over her, really."

"We need the skim back, Jesus. If you go after her, maybe she'll live. If I have to send somebody from my crew, my higher ups will notice. I'll have to report to them. They'll require things to be done that neither of us want to happen. Not to Lily. I need somebody I can trust, off the chain, but not so off the chain that they'll come at Lily heavy. Take care of this and we're cool."

"Why so generous, Denny?"

"You're like a brother and Lily was like a sister-in-law. I don't want her dead. I just need the money back. Whatever's left of it. I hear she's frugal."

"I don't remember her that way."

"I need what she has. It'll be a lot. As soon as you're up and around, I need you to go get it."

You watch Denny's eyes. Each blink takes a fraction of a second too long. He's lying about something.

"You need the money for something big. You owe a lot of money or you're going to use it for something off The

Machine's books. You lose big betting on the ponies?"

He stares at you for what seems like a full minute and hardly blinks at all. "You in or out?"

Maybe he'll kill you, after all.

No.

No, he won't. Not after going to all this effort to save you. Not yet. Big Denny needs you to be his outside talent.

You give him a warm smile. A real smile. In the end, you tell yourself, no one's smarter than Jesus. But if you heal, save Lily and somehow manage to bring him the money? You're still you and Denny is still Denny. You can get a new switchblade and a new SIG Sauer, but you're stuck with your luck.

Go ahead. Follow orders again. Save Lily. You can even throw Denny a "sir" or two to make him feel good. You tell yourself all the time you're the smart ninja, but you know if your life was really a movie, you wouldn't live past the first reel. No matter what you do, no one will really see you as the good guy. You tell yourself you're bigger than The Beatles. You kid yourself that no one is harder than Jesus. Like the Olympic motto, you're faster, higher, stronger. The lies make you brave, but you know that you're on a one way trip that doesn't end with a little house surrounded by a white picket fence.

God put a gun in your hand and he won't let you put it down. No choices. There is no free will. Every time you try to use your will, the bill is too high and you pay in blood. In the end, no one will be deader than Jesus.

It's time for a new identity. It's time to grow up and try to stop talking to yourself. It's especially time to stop telling yourself lies to get through each day. But if you can't be you, anymore, who will you be?

"It's always out of the frying pan, into the napalm with you, Jesus. In or out, man? I need to know now, 'cuz if you're out, you know you gotta be all the way out."

"Just like the first time, doing that guy in Wanton, New Jersey."

"Huh? Who?"

"I haven't forgotten...sir." You smile wider at Denny. "The Divine Assassin is in. Goodbye, Hollywood Jesus."

**There's more to come in 2015.
Jesus Diaz returns in**

*Resurrected
The Divine Assassin's Playbook
by Robert Chazz Chute*

*In the meantime, don't miss Bigger Than Jesus
and Higher Than Jesus.
Or read all of the first three books in the series
in
The Divine Assassin's Playbook, Omnibus
Edition.*

If you'd like to get a glimpse of Jesus Diaz as a mature, more professional assassin, you can find him in *The Inevitable*, the story that started his character, in the short story collection, *Self-help for Stoners*. You'll find Jesus is more polished, but things still go awry. *Self-help for Stoners* also gives you Legs and Chill together in the first story, revisiting the regrets of her past in Poeticule Bay, Maine.

* * *

Poeticule Bay shows up in *Murders Among Dead Trees* and the *This Plague of Days Series*, as well.

ABOUT THE AUTHOR

Titles By Robert Chazz Chute

Fiction

Bigger Than Jesus
Higher Than Jesus
Hollywood Jesus, Rise of the Divine Assassin
The Divine Assassin's Playbook, Omnibus Edition
Self-help for Stoners
Murders Among Dead Trees
This Plague of Days, Season One
This Plague of Days, Season Two
This Plague of Days, Season, Season Three
This Plague of Days, Omnibus Edition
Intense Violence, Bizarre Themes
The Haunting Lessons

Poetry
The Little Book of Braingasms

* * *
Non-fiction

Crack the Indie Author Code (Book One)
Write Your Book: Aspire to Inspire (Book Two)
Six Seconds

Available now!

Intense Violence, Bizarre Themes ~ In this quirky and quick crime novel, our hero returns home to New York, the prodigal son to a father who doesn't know him anymore. If you like the *Hit Man Series* (or *The Big Lebowski*), you'll love this funny, thrilling story about absent minds, missing gems, missing persons and missing out.

The Haunting Lessons, Book One of the Ghosts and Demons Series ~ In this funny and fast-paced dark fantasy, a young woman named Tamara Smythe from Iowa has her life planned out. When tragedy strikes, she discovers she has abilities others only dream of, but seeing what others cannot is a curse. Soon Tam is off to New York to discover the Secret City of the Unseen where an army prepares to do battle. Read *The Haunting Lessons* and learn the first 88 lessons that may help you survive Armageddon.

About the Author

Chazz has a degree in journalism and is a podcaster, former magazine columnist and features writer. He is a graduate of the Banff Publishing Workshop and has won seven writing awards. He's a Canadian living in Other London. Say hi on Twitter @rchazzchute & @AssassinsPlayBk.

**To discover new book releases, blogs and podcasts from Chazz,
please visit AllThatChazz.com and subscribe to the newsletter.**